I0525828

CALLING THE PRIESTESS HOME

Book One Of The Priestess Chronicles

JULIEN DUBROW

Published By Julien DuBrow Ventures
San Francisco, California

Published by Julien DuBrow Ventures: www.JulienDuBrow.com

Book Cover Images by Helena Nelson-Reed: www.fine-art-studios.com

Map by Brenden Hickey: rednecter@hotmail.com

ISBN: 978-1-7352164-0-9

First Printing, 2018
Second Printing, 2020

For my beloved grandmother, Roz,
who has blessed my life with her presence.

"She is more beautiful than the sun,
and above all the order of stars;
being compared with light, she is found before it…"

The Book Of Wisdom, ca. 100 B.C.

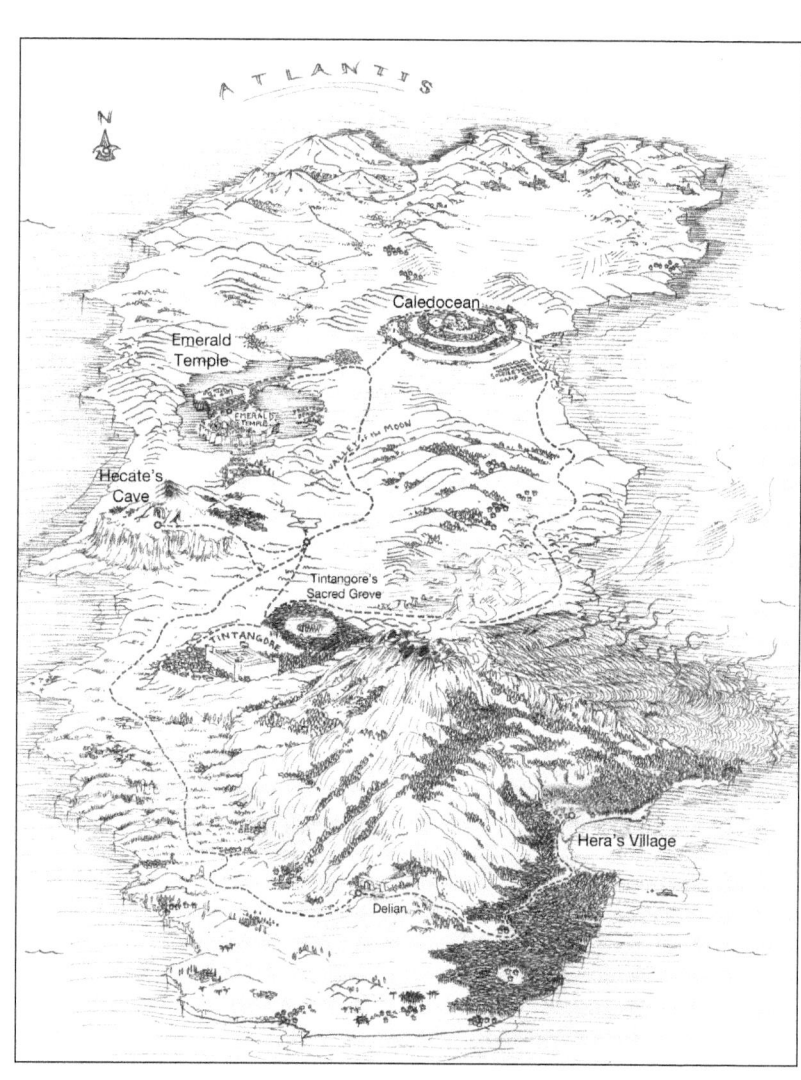

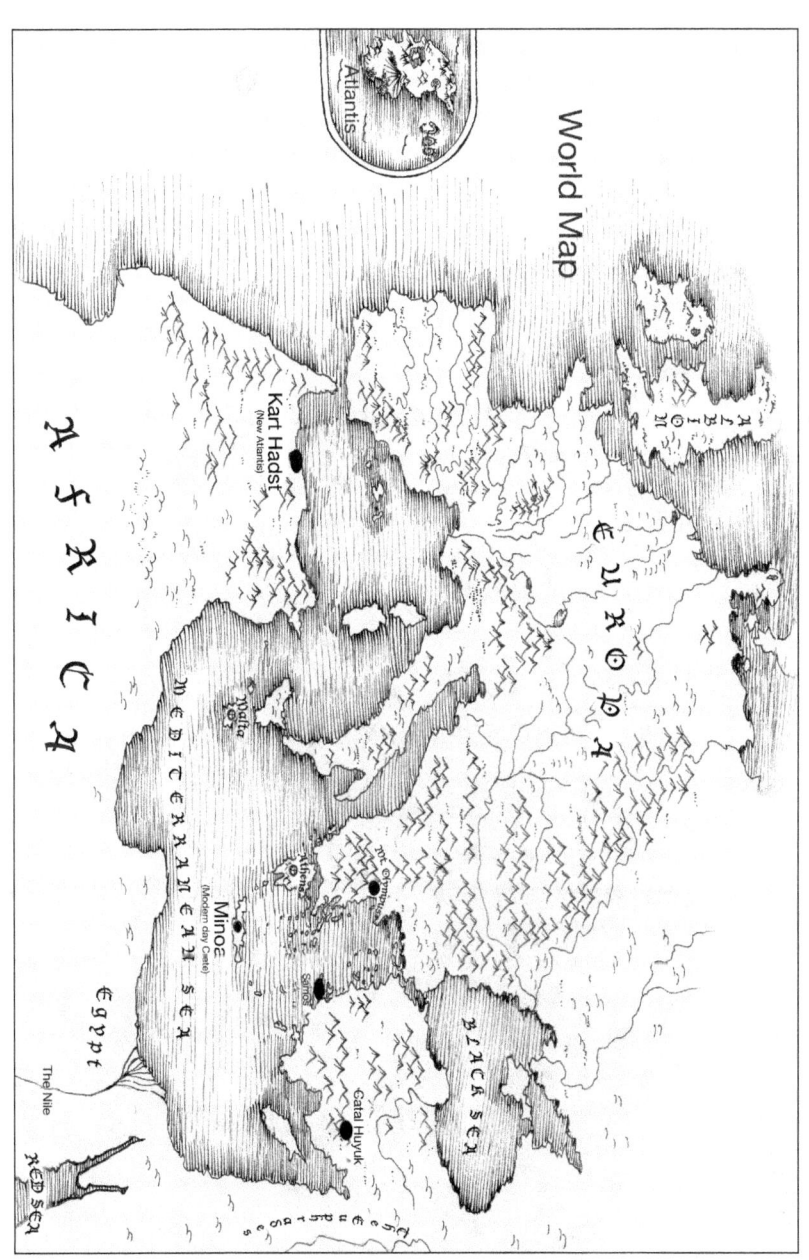

World Map

Atlantis

EUROPA

Kar Hadst
(New Atlantis)

AFRICA

Malta

MEDITERRANEAN SEA

Mt. Olympus

Minoe
(Modern day Crete)

Samos

BLACK SEA

Catal Huyuk

Egypt

The Nile

RED SEA

O royal Hera of majestic mien
aerial-formed, divine, Zeus's blessed queen.

Thy throne in the bosom of cerulean air
the race of mortals is thy constant care.

Mother of the elements, from thee alone
birthing all things our mortal life is known.

Come blessed Goddess, famed almighty queen
with aspect kind, rejoicing and serene.

Orphic Hymn 16
Adapted from translation by Thomas Taylor

HERA SPEAKS

I HAVE NOT ALWAYS BEEN IMMORTAL.

There was a time before your own histories were born that I was flesh and blood, able to grow old and even die.

There was a time when you knew me by name. In Greece, I came to you with my consorts and companions, and you worshipped me as a Goddess. In antiquity, I rose to fame, bringing you the ancient teachings and their wisdom.

But you did not love me for that.

It was Zeus you honored, the patriarch, who turned your world from its mystical design and pressed you to betray the night, the moon and the feminine divine. You lost sight of your true nature.

Ah, but who am I to say such things? I, who ran away from it all, hidden here, in my Minoan cave, for millennia, watching the rise and fall of your civilizations, as if in a dream. It is I, Hera, queen of the Greek Gods, who has betrayed my conscience and its call.

I am ready now to tell you my story. This is no fiction, so do not read these words with a careless heart, expecting entertainment alone. For in the telling, I will unearth myself, and the truth you have come to believe as only a myth. My words will change you. There is no place to hide now, no island, or cave to disappear into.

The time has come to speak the truth.

The first story is not my own. It is a dark beginning that belongs to us all. Later you will understand how I know these things, how it is as much a memory to me, as a vision of the past. It seems right that I will begin with the story of the priestess who came before me, and whose story lives on within us all.

This is what happened... I saw it in the flames, and it is true.

It was a dimly lit night, and the cave was cold, but the young woman had lit a small fire, which gave a little light and warmth. It had been raining all night, and water still dripped from the mouth of the cave, soaking the green earth below. All through the night, she'd kept watch. Several times, restless, she'd pulled her cloak over her head, and walked up the hill to look down on the temple, in the valley below. She could see the warm glow of fires burning behind the temple walls and in the braziers of the sleeping rooms, as if all was well. She had longed to be there, standing by her sister priestesses as they prepared for what was to come.

Now, dawn approached, and the rain had stopped. She threw dirt on the little fire at the mouth of the cave and gripped her blade walking out again, this time into the grove below. The earth was still damp, and a thick mist had risen. A soft light filled the sky and the wet leaves on the trees shimmered. When she reached the meeting place, she moved to the pile of stones unearthing the bag that carried the temple treasures. She had wrapped the sacred things in dull wool, and rough linen, and wore an old fisherman's cloak. The gilded emerald upon her wrist, which she'd sworn to wear always, was covered in a tarnished metal band, and torn strips of linen, for she was the High Priestess' daughter, and if they caught her, they would surely kill her. She was just sixteen.

She heard movement in the grove. Her body tensed, but trained as a warrior priestess, she did not move. With a hand on the hilt of her blade, she drew in her breath, reaching out with her intuitive senses.

She sent her mind into the silence and stillness of the grove, waiting. Then she felt them, the 13 High Priestesses, of the Emerald Temple, of Lemuria, waiting just at the edge of the glen. She put a hand to her lips whistling softly, the sound of a morning bird, sharp, and sweet.

And the call was answered.

She smiled, stepping forward as the group of women moved out of the trees towards her. They were wrapped in dark cloaks that covered their heads and shrouded their faces. The leader was small and slight. As she approached, she lifted her hand and pulled back her hood.

"Mother," the young woman said embracing the small figure. "No one saw you?"

"It's hard to say. The rain made it difficult to travel, and they've been patrolling the roads day and night. We had to come through the forest, which was slow and now the sun is already rising."

"Mother, I imagined worse. Come," the young woman said. "We must hurry, the ship will leave on the morning tide. I have everything arranged."

Signaling to the others she turned to the well-worn path that would lead them to the cove and the ship that waited.

She kept her mind focused, staying away from thoughts of those that had been left behind, her sister priestesses that would give their lives this day to hold the temple from the priests and warriors that gathered at its gates. It was a grave responsibility she had been given. She must ensure the survival of the temple by smuggling out its elders, those that could rebuild the temple if they could safely land on the shores of Atlantis.

The women made their way to the base of the hill and the small cove with its crescent shore. The sun was now breaking the horizon, and she could see the ship still anchored in the bay. She moved quickly to the outrigger canoe that she'd left hidden in the brush signaling the elders to follow. Swiftly they took their places around the craft, preparing to bring it to the sea, but the High Priestess held up her hand and stopped them.

Turning to her daughter, she whispered, "We're not alone."

A moment later, the young woman felt it too; the inescapable sense that someone was watching them. She reached for her blade, but her mother reached out her hand.

"There are too many," her mother said. "It is just as the dreamers have foretold."

The elders circled around her.

"You know what must be done," one said to the High Priestess. She put a hand on the young woman's shoulder. "We will watch over her," she said.

At this, the young woman startled, but before she could respond her mother reached for the emerald medallion around her neck and placed it over her daughter's head.

"No, no, hush, you must listen to me now," the High Priestess said to her daughter. Raising her hands to her child's cheeks, she spoke strong and low.

"I know you haven't understood why you were chosen to protect the temple in this way. I know you are a warrior priestess, and too young, and want to stand with your sisters defending the temple."

The young woman reached for the emerald at her chest, confused. Kindness emanated from the medallion, spreading its warmth over her breast.

"Mother," she tried to say, but the High Priestess went on.

"Listen! This is unfolding as was prophesized. You are here because you are my daughter and you are the last of our lineage. The wisdom that lives within me lives within you. The innate gifts of our line must continue. Look to the fire within you, my daughter. Live by the code of peace, justice, and truth!"

There was a faint and familiar sound on the wind. The young woman snapped her head to the far side of the beach.

"Horses!" she said. "That will mean soldiers."

"To the boat!" her mother commanded.

The young woman took her place at the bow of the canoe leading the priestesses as they half lifted, half dragged the craft down the shore to the water's edge. Plunging into the sea she pulled it into the water. She could feel the power of the horses charging down the beach as she threw the bag of sacred objects into the bow, then turned to help the elders into their places. As the sound of men's voices rose up behind her, she looked back to the beach, realizing all was lost. The soldiers were too close. She would not get the priestesses out to sea in time.

And then she heard it, the unmistakable hum, rushing, shimmering upon the invisible currents of life: it was the sound of her mother's bees. She looked frantically at the faces in the boat, but her mother was not among them.

In that moment it all became clear.

Turning back to the shore, she saw her mother, the last High Priestess of Lemuria, keeper of the sacred symbol of wisdom, Lady of the Bees. The High Priestess stood on the shore between the soldiers and her daughter, hands lifted high as she intoned the sacred sound, calling to the queen bee, calling to the hive. As the soldiers bore down on her, the bees came. In a sacred swarm, they rose up around her. The horses shrieked and reared, throwing soldiers to the ground. Some men staggered to their feet, dropping their blades, swatting at the bees, while others were crushed beneath their mounts.

Through the chaos, the young woman lifted the last elder into the boat. Looking back, she watched, helpless, as the High Priestess was finally struck down.

"My heart to your heart," she whispered as her mother's body fell to the sand.

Turning to the canoe, she took hold of the stern, pushing with all her strength to move it out to sea. Without looking back, she pulled herself in and took up the last paddle. Leaning into each stroke with pain, and purpose, she pulled hard alongside the elders, moving the craft toward the ship that would carry them to Atlantis.

CHAPTER ONE

IN THE SPRING OF MY SEVENTEENTH YEAR, I went out to hunt the boar.

This was in the wet jungle of my childhood home, on the Eastern shore of Atlantis, and these were the last decades before the island was overtaken by the sea.

I awoke at dawn, and slipped quietly from my mat by the hearth, pulled my pack over my shoulder, and crept across the koa wood floors hoping I wouldn't wake my parents. As I pushed the *tapa* cloth away from the front door, a cool, colorless mist kissed my skin. I smiled and stepped barefoot onto the ground. The earth was cold, and I moved quickly across it, over the small bridge that crossed the stream, to the path that would lead me down to the village, to my friend, Artemis, and the hunting party she'd gathered to initiate me. As I reached the head of the trail, I heard Father's voice calling me. I stopped and looked back. He was already moving toward me through the grass.

A light flashed from within the house behind him, and I knew Mother was stoking the morning fire inside. Our dwelling was long and thin. Its roofline flared out like wings in the tradition of Father's people from across the sea. Even with the soft orange glow of the flame within, it seemed to be a lonely and solitary sight, set back so far among the hills above the village. I was eager to be away from its tranquility. My legs quivered with the desire to step onto the familiar path and run to the hunt, but I held myself fast as Father approached. His pace was slow and mindful as if his steps were a prayer. He held something in his hand.

"Father," I said, bowing my head in respect as he crossed the bridge. "I'll be late—"

"I won't keep you long, Hera," he said and held out a thinly sheathed blade to me. "I want you to take this. Your mother has had a dream."

I looked up sharply. Mother's dreams were to be taken seriously.

"What sort of dream?" I asked. Father shook his head.

"Your destiny is written in your bones, my daughter," he began, his voice so soft that I moved toward him to hear. "And it won't be altered by a dream."

He smiled at me, pulling out the blade. "It's very old, and the passing on of such a blade is a tradition within our families. My mother gave me one like it when I took the ship that brought me to the shores of Atlantis. Your mother was given this one when she left her people and came away with me." He paused and looked me in the eye. "She tells me you used it in the dream."

I held the knife in my palm and moved my hand over it. Warmth passed through me. I looked up into Father's black eyes and grinned.

"I never thought you'd give me a weapon—"

"Not a weapon," he cut me off. "A blade for defense."

I nodded and slid it into my pack. The sky was now dim with light. "I'll be safe," I said.

He lifted his brows slightly as if in assent. I knew how hard it was for him to let me go. He and Mother didn't approve of hunting. They couldn't understand why I did such a thing, but they did not try to stop me.

We stood quietly for another moment until I leaned forward and kissed his cheek.

"Thank you," I whispered in his ear.

My words softened his reserve, and when I stood back, I was pleased to see a small smile pull on his lips. As quickly as it appeared his face became a cool mask again. He nodded sharply toward the trailhead and then turned to walk back to the house.

I slung my pack over my shoulder and headed down. Wet ferns brushed my ankles as I moved quickly around the familiar bends, over mossy rocks, and through the thick fragrances of waking flowers. I smelled the smoke of early morning fires as I reached the bottom of the hill.

The village sat in a long, thick crescent beneath the banyans that lined the beach. I made my way to the trail behind the huts, and the larger family compounds made of stone and mud, through banana leaves and sweet ginger until I reached the freshwater pool where Artemis waited.

A small fire glowed inside a rough-hewn stone, and an open gourd sat on the ground beside it. The sky was filled with muted light, and I could just make out her tall, familiar form. A spear was thrust into the ground beside her. I smiled and moved toward her quickly, but she put up her hand and stopped me as I reached the fire.

"Slowly, Hera," she said, her voice soft. "Your initiation begins here, before the hunt. We have a ritual."

I cringed as she said the word, taking a deep breath to still myself. A reserved demeanor was not natural to me, and I had always avoided rites and rituals whenever I could; such things bored me.

"But Artemis," I said as she moved toward me, slowly, as if walking through a dream. "We'll keep the hunters waiting!"

"The hunters won't allow you to join them if your instinctive abilities haven't been awakened through our rites, Hera," she replied, stepping into the light of the fire before me.

I stared at her for a moment, surprised to see her bare arms colored with designs, in a style I'd seen on the healers and priestesses from neighboring villages. The clear imprint of a bow and arrow, Artemis's symbol, was painted in coal upon her brow, shimmering against her dark skin. Her eyes were rimmed with black as well, and her long, dark hair fell loose to her waist.

I shifted my weight from one foot to the other and dropped my pack at my feet as I realized the seriousness of her intent.

"Every profession has its rites," she continued. "Your initiation as a huntress begins here, Hera, with me."

I stood very still. Artemis's tone was severe. While I had become used to her reserve long ago, she'd never taken such a stance with me before. Even on those occasions when she had taken me deep into the green, learning to track beasts and catch fowl, I had only experienced her gentle direction and constant love. I calmed myself, remembering that then I had been a girl; today I would become a woman.

Artemis moved her hand toward the fire and let loose some powder that made the flame crackle and leap, sending its warmth over my skin. She took another step toward me, very close. Reaching for my tunic, she loosened the pin at my shoulder, and the cloth fell away from my collarbone. My hair was tied back in a long, thick braid, leaving my face exposed. I didn't move. I held my breath as she dipped her hands into the large pot at her side and removed them covered with dark, thick clay—the red earth the hunters painted their bodies with before a ritual hunt.

"I am Artemis," she began, her voice low but strong. She held her hands open before me. "I am the daughter of Leto from the clan of Coeus, the hunter, and I initiate you, Hera, into the art of the hunt."

Her hands were cold on my skin, and the mud was damp as she pressed it first against my chest then streaked my cheeks with her thumbs. My heart raced.

She signaled me to kneel down beside her and ran her palms across the ground as if it were her skin. Then, like a snake striking, she snapped toward me, thrusting her hands behind my neck, drawing me to her, hard and sharp. I shivered.

She whispered, "You *belong* to the earth."

The intensity of her voice moved through me. The strength of her hands seemed to pulse into my bones. For a moment I felt disoriented. Suddenly, Artemis was no longer my friend, my mentor or my idol, but a transformed figure with a strong and almost brutal instinct. This was an unfamiliar part of her. I was mesmerized by it.

Artemis was older than I was, and there had always been a side of her that I didn't understand. She often disappeared into the jungle for days at a time to hunt, pray, and be alone. I had tried to know this other side of her, but she hadn't let me come that close. No matter how devoted I had been, she would not let me know this part of her.

When she was old enough to take a lover, I was jealous, knowing she would choose women, for she'd always made that clear. Being too young and insecure, I feared I would never know her as genuinely as one of them.

Now, I understood that would never happen, for here, in the instinctual nature of her being, was the origin of her female power, and she was sharing it with *me*.

I smiled deeply.

Artemis chanted long and slow. The tone drew all my senses toward it. I caught my breath and pulled back slightly. The blackness of her pupils responded to my movement. Her hands tightened on my shoulders. I stood perfectly still, watching, as her dark skin changed to the reddish color of the earth beneath us. Her carved features were transforming; for a moment she became the jungle cat, her large eyes slanting, filled with bodily desire. I could almost smell blood.

"I speak to the invisible force that gives you breath," she began.

The fire leapt.

"I call to your eternal nature." My body swayed slightly to some distant beat. "I call to your innate gifts, Hera, *awaken!*"

I caught the scent of ancient clay on her skin and felt a deep, instinctual urge to lie down and roll upon the ground, to cover my body with another layer of skin. I shivered, and my head felt light. I sensed Artemis's power and determination to awaken something inside me, but I felt a conflict within myself. The far away sound that seemed to be moving my body grew louder; I wanted to lift my hands to my ears. Artemis didn't seem to notice it at all. She continued to chant, holding me fast.

Suddenly, I became aware of the strong pull from a force beside me, a steady, warm rush as if the flame in the fire pit was moving in my direction past the stone that encircled it. I turned and looked into the fire.

A riotous flash of light.

Burning in my bones.

A profound, unfamiliar force rose up through my torso as if it was claiming me.

These things overtook me.

For a moment I enjoyed the rush of power. As Artemis continued her ritual before me, I felt the distinct awakening of my senses. I'd heard other hunters speak of such things in their rites of passage, but they always described it as a sense of awe and humility in the face of a vast, feminine force. What I felt was both feminine and masculine; a balanced, persuasive surging that did not come from outside myself. This power came from deep within.

My body trembled slightly, and I shut my eyes. Artemis's voice filled the space around me.

"The huntress awakens!" she cried. "That which has been forgotten is remembered!"

My body shuddered hard. The heat expanded from the center of an unseen flame that sparked in my belly. It bellowed up and out, filling my limbs with a luxurious sense of authority.

"Artemis," my voice was hushed as if grasping for sound. I felt the new thrill of this imaginative vigor that filled me. "Artemis, the heat—" but I didn't finish for the sensation rushed down my arms and filled my palms with such intensity I gasped.

Artemis paused in her recitation. She released her firm grip and slid her hands gently to my wrists, which I realized were shaking.

"We're awakening the hunter's intuition," she said in a soothing voice. Despite her words, I knew the heat was something else, something much more profound that had been hidden inside me.

Warmth rose up my bones, something red and rough that wanted no part in banal things. I felt it call to something sacred in me, and an eternal voice seemed to answer it: *Hera, you are my daughter!* I heard the voice as certainly as if it was my own and my body trembled. *You have my gift. Hold the light!*

I clenched my fists.

"Hera, what is it?" Artemis's voice was sharp.

I shook my head as the heat faded and the voice with it. My throat was hot and dry. I licked my lips instinctively. I struggled to get my body under control, to open my eyes in her direction. I forced a smile, trying to shake the unnerving sensations that lingered. I could see by the look on Artemis's face that something had gone wrong and this was not the reaction she'd expected from me in the Huntress' initiation. I stood up straighter and commanded my body to stop its shaking, wary of the possibility that she would not take me with her on the hunt. I didn't care whether I understood what had happened to me. All that mattered now was the overwhelming power that filled my limbs. I was not going to be left behind.

The sun had broken the horizon. Artemis stared into my eyes for a long time as if searching for some missing piece. I held her gaze until she seemed satisfied. She drew me into an embrace. I could still feel the sweat from the inner heat, slick on my skin, even beneath the clay.

"Hera, are you alright?" Artemis finally asked as she drew me away and held me at arm's length. "You're very warm. I've never seen anyone awaken to the ritual so strongly."

I nodded with assurance and again forced a smile. I

looked at the path that would take us to the mountain and the hunting party beyond and felt the urge to set my feet upon it.

"The ritual has served its purpose. Something has been born in me," I said with confidence, to appease her. I reached quickly for my pack and stepped out of her reach. "I'm ready, Artemis. Take me to the boar."

Artemis and I walked in silence. The jungle was slow to wake. Her Macaws lulled in their nests and monkeys stayed silent in the trees, watching us as we passed. We pushed our way through ancient groves of wild mango, past anteaters and the prints of jungle cats until the mountain slope gave way to a long plateau of turquoise. Much higher up I could see it merge with the jagged mustard lip of the volcano.

The plateau was drier and red-soiled with a fern-carpeted quiet, which led to the open woodlands and dried up streams. Here the wild pigs wallowed during the day, rooting amongst the leaf litter and damp soil for food. As we came over the first ridge, we caught sight of the rest of the hunting party, and their packs which were strewn along the base of a gentle hill. Most of the hunters were face down near the top, their spears at the ready. Coeus, Artemis's grandfather, and Apollo, her twin brother, waited for us at the bottom.

When we reached them, Coeus smiled broadly and nodded in my direction. I grinned back to signal my readiness. I could still feel remnants of the ritual heat in my limbs and was eager to make my first real kill.

Coeus signaled us silently and pointed to the hill. Artemis nodded and pulled the top of her bow down hard with her right hand, her foot bracing the bottom as she laced the bowstring in one graceful movement. Apollo approached us then and handed me my spear. I took it from him and hoisted it to my shoulder. The weight in my palm felt right, and the heat surged through me again. I struggled with a strange and compelling desire to thrust the spear.

I set down my pack and pulled out the blade my father had given me earlier and tied it to my ankle with pride. Apollo knelt down beside me, running his fingers over the carved handle.

"Dragons entwined," he sounded surprised.

"My father gave it to me this morning; I want to wear it in his honor."

Artemis stared down at us but was silent. Apollo was mesmerized by its design.

"I've seen this symbol before, Hera," he said, "when I was studying at the great temple of the healers. Dragons are the symbol of healing, immortality and the priestesses of—"

"Apollo," Artemis said sternly, putting her hand on his shoulder. "It's time."

We stood up and climbed the hill. I stayed close to Artemis's side, eager and excited. We dropped to our knees and then our bellies as we neared the top of the ridge to take cover. We lay behind the sparse brush, low to the ground. Down the slight incline, I saw a large group of sows with their piglets just born in the early spring. We wouldn't hunt mothers or the young. We sought the male yearlings, scattered on the outskirts of the party, their short, bristly coats and undefined tusks making them easier marks. The older boars—the wild fathers—would join the pack in the fall to mate and fight. Their skin would be thick and more difficult to pierce, their snouts short and tusks long. They lived on their own, growing as long as a man, weighing more than three. Only the most experienced hunters would track these beasts.

Artemis slid up to my right side and pointed across the field. There, a small group of young males, recognizable by their dark, black coats, mingled in the grass. I gripped my spear. Apollo slid up to my left side.

"Stay close to me," he whispered. I turned, surprised. I was about to protest, but Artemis touched my hand lightly.

"I can't stay with you," she said. "I will be here on the hill, calling the boar close. Follow him, Hera."

She didn't wait for me to respond. Silently, she slid over the peak of the ridge on her belly and came to rest in the thick shrub. She signaled to Coeus and then began a low, steady chant, soft and eerie, that floated up over our heads and mingled with the light mist. The sound moved down onto the plateau as if being pushed by an invisible draft. Abruptly, the animals looked up, until the sows grunted gently, and the piglets moved in close to their mothers' bodies. The male yearlings didn't run but lifted their heads and pricked their ears while standing rigid and alert.

I watched Artemis rise from the brush, her hands outstretched to them. She swayed gently. Still, her song was delicate and low. I was stirred by her beauty, the gentle curve of her hips as they moved, her muscular legs reaching up as if they were part of the earth itself.

I felt Apollo move next to me and in a moment I was crouched at his side, my spear poised on my shoulder. As Artemis continued chanting, the herd of males moved, slowly at first, as if in a trance, and then with speed as they trotted toward us on the slope. The sows stirred as they passed, making for the trees. The piglets followed, scampering through the brush, raising a small cloud of red dust that rose above us in the breeze. For a moment, Artemis and the field below were obscured. Then the haze lifted and the boars charged toward us. Coeus's voice rang out, and the hunters ran in a long, sweeping line down the hill. I felt Apollo's hand on my back, pushing me forward and then my legs moved with a desire all their own. I lifted my spear and cried out as the others did, a long, shrill sound that joined with their voices, pulling the pigs up short. Suddenly, as if waking from a dream, they pricked their ears and grunted, most turning toward the trees to flee.

Apollo, who ran close at my side, lifted his hand and pointed to a small creature that lay straight ahead.

"Take aim and throw!" he cried, his spear held low in a defensive posture, protecting me.

A surge of defiance ran through me. I felt the strange, hot desire of the ritual fire burning in my belly as I waved my hand and shook him off, veering suddenly away to the right. I had spotted a much more prominent and older beast, which had just dodged one of Coeus's spears and was headed for the tall brush. Because I hadn't stopped to make my kill, I was almost between the boar and the tree line. Pushing myself even harder, I ran ten paces and launched my spear. I was too young to be afraid.

CHAPTER TWO

My spear flew straight towards its target through the air. For a moment, my body slowed. My breath froze in my chest as an unfamiliar quiet filled my ears. Then, a strange magic enfolded me.

I heard the tip of my spear pierce the animal's pelt.

A shocking pain streamed through my skin. The boar screamed, slicing the silence, and I fell to my knees, clutching at my chest. I tasted blood in my mouth, and I gasped for breath as the beast spun around, flailing its head in my direction.

Only then did I realize the actual size of the creature. This was no yearling. It was a full grown boar.

He sighted me.

I could feel the intensity of his gaze, the raw recognition of his death penetrating my body. I shook. My spear wagged between its shoulders, but when he moved toward me, it fell to the ground.

It came to me suddenly that this is what it meant to be mortal, to be vulnerable and beyond strength. I faced my death, and I knew it.

As the creature bore down on me, head bent, his sharp, white tusks directed at my chest, I felt my body go still and numb.

And then the pain was gone.

At the moment the beast would have me, I heard a sharp whistle behind my ear and then another and another and all of a sudden the boar reared up before me and was pushed back by a fury of Artemis's arrows. He spun around and grunted, the shafts breaking on the ground, and then he thundered past me in her direction. I turned in time to see Artemis throw down her bow and pull an arrow from the pouch on her pack. As the boar reached her, even as it tore into the flesh of her leg and pulled her to the ground, Artemis thrust the arrow into its skin. I wanted to cry out, but then I heard Father's voice, clear and calm as if he were standing beside me, "You used the blade in the dream."

In a moment I was on my feet moving toward Artemis, my hand gripped tight around the dragon hilt. On the ground, trapped beneath the boar, she made a horrible, red scream. I leaped into the air and came down hard on the boar's back, driving my blade in deep. I rolled off the animal as it turned sharply with a long, final shriek and then fell to the ground at my feet, dead.

The moment held me in a web of terror, and a thick fog seemed to linger between my body and the action it should take next. I stood very still, breathing hard, my hands covered in blood. A chill swept over me as I stared at the boar and Artemis's limp form beside it.

In a moment Apollo was at her side. Then Coeus approached, throwing down his spears and kneeling to lift her. Apollo held up his hand to stop him. She was broken and losing too much blood.

A hunter came with Apollo's bag and a waterskin. He pulled out strips of cloth and tied them around the top of her leg, just above the gash and then tried to press her torn flesh together. She shrieked. A wave of nausea rose in my stomach, and I fought to push it down. There was a deep, sharp sound and I realized that Coeus was blowing the conch, signaling the other hunters to gather. Still, I stood, unable to move.

As the others approached, Coeus shouted directions.

"Andros, take the men to the tree line and get us some poles. We'll have to carry her out. Dameon, we'll need more water to clean the leg!"

Apollo pulled dried herbs from his bag and began to chew them. Then he bound the poultice into a cloth and tried to tie it around the wound. He turned to me.

"Hera," he said as if to direct me, but his voice seemed far away. "Hera, come help me."

I nodded but still didn't move.

"Hera!" Apollo shouted, and then again, "Hera!"

Coeus was on his knees holding his granddaughter's hand. She lay there quiet now, as if dead.

I stood there numbly staring until Coeus got to his feet and took sharp hold of my arm.

"Wake up, girl!" he cried.

My body trembled with the force of his voice.

"It's my fault," I gasped, my voice breaking into tears.

"The boar was too big!" Coeus continued harshly.

"Yes," I said. "I should've run back toward Apollo and led the boar away. Apollo had a spear. He would've made the kill!"

I wrung my hands with the horrible certainty of my mistake. The sickening realization that I couldn't undo this thing took hold of my body, and I shook. "I should've run, but I couldn't move," I said in a small voice.

Apollo pressed his hands to the wound, but they were covered in Artemis's blood.

"I can't stop the bleeding," he said desperately.

"But you have the gift of light and healing in your hands, Apollo!" Coeus cried again.

Apollo's voice choked. "I can't mend this wound."

I shook my head and wept. The heat that had spurred me on earlier was now a growing numbness.

"I couldn't move," I repeated to Artemis's limp form. My chest ached. I wanted to reach out and touch her, but I was shaking too hard. "I felt a sharp pain when my spear landed and then I couldn't move!"

Apollo looked up at me as I said this.

"What?" he said, "What did you say, Hera?"

"There was so much pain," I went on frantically, "and I couldn't move even when he charged me."

"Hera," Apollo said, but I was weeping and lost in horror and my grief. "Hera!" I heard his voice, but I couldn't respond.

Apollo turned to Coeus and said something in a low tone. The older man let out a breath. He turned to me and took hold of my shoulders, shaking me hard.

"Hera, child!" he said.

I only wept more. I heard my name again, but this time softer, and then in a short, abrupt movement he pulled me to his chest and wrapped me in his arms.

"It's going to be okay," he said, his voice filled with emotion. "Listen to me, Hera. Apollo needs your help now. Our Artemis may still live through this day."

I heard his words and felt the strength in his body. He moved me gently toward Apollo who was covering Artemis with a long robe. Her face was pale, and she lay very still.

"We have to keep her warm," Apollo said. "She's still breathing, and there are no other broken places. It's the bleeding we have to control."

My tears slowed. I knelt down at Apollo's side.

"Hera, I've heard your story before," Apollo said hurriedly. "In the Temple of Healers, there was a group whose ability with the light was powerful, but this also made them sensitive. They could be overwhelmed and taken by disease, or the death they attended. They had to be trained to keep themselves whole in the face of another's pain. But, Hera, their ability to heal is potent."

He removed his hands from his sister's wound and swiftly took my palms into his own. The heat in my belly leapt to life as when Artemis had sung her chant. I felt it surge through my arms as if racing toward the oil that would turn it to flame. Suddenly, my palms filled with warmth and Apollo let go.

"Yes," he murmured. He pulled my hands toward his sister's leg, and I tried not to recoil from the blood as I let him press my palms to the wound. "Try to mend the flesh, Hera," he begged. "Imagine the bleeding slowing to a stop."

I tried to keep my palms on Artemis's wound, but when I felt the fresh, warm blood, I pulled them away despite myself.

I felt Coeus lean down beside me, his firm hands on my shoulders. The hunters had gathered around.

"Love," Apollo said, his voice choked as Artemis's blood ran fresh from the wound. "Just focus on your love for her, Hera. That is the only thing that ever really heals anyone."

He looked down at his sister for a long moment. Tears filled his eyes and spilled down his cheeks. As I followed his gaze to Artemis's familiar face tears rose in my eyes as well. I looked back to her leg and laid my hands on the wound.

I love you, I thought. I shut my eyes and pictured her face, smiling at me. *I love you so.*

The heat in my hands seemed to soften, and the blood slowed. I heard Apollo's voice urging me on. I felt my heart beating hard and used it's fervor to pull Artemis closer to me. *I love you,* I thought again and again, until my mind stilled. *I've always loved you.*

The sensation of warm water moved through my limbs, and my hands felt like chalices of fluent love. In another moment my heart loosened itself in my breast and sang love songs through my veins. The deep, penetrating sound resonated through my palms and I rushed along with it. Into her flesh, I went, drawn deep down into a stillness and peace that lived in her bones.

Around us, I could hear the muted sounds of activity as Coeus directed the others to build a stretcher and gather their things. I felt the movement of her body as they lifted her gently onto the bed and wrapped us both in warm robes.

At some point Artemis twitched, letting out a delirious sound, but Apollo was quick to soothe her, his voice low and firm in her ear. Her body trembled, and I felt an invisible force push me away from the silence within her. It felt as if her body had detected that the boundary had been broached and that I lingered too intimately. A cold, damp chill moved over me and even as I realized it to be the hands of death welling up to push me away, I steeled myself against it.

Artemis's body shook harder despite Apollo's healing hands on her as well. Then, an unexpected instinct rose up inside of me, and I pulled my heart's healing song back inside myself, bringing Artemis's heart with me. I imagined my arms around her, my voice soothing, and in a moment, she quieted and lay still.

"Good, Hera," Apollo said as he placed his hands gently on mine, lending me his strength.

For a moment I felt him pull me in as I had pulled in Artemis and the three of us were bathed in a warm peace.

Then, Coeus was washing away the blood, cleaning our hands and Artemis's wound. Fresh linen was laid over it, but a thin red line had already appeared.

"Hera we'll have to keep our hands on her leg as we go," Apollo said. He glanced up at his grandfather, his brow furrowed. "It's a long way, and you'd better send ahead for a surgeon."

I nodded and placed my hands back in their position, but my legs felt weak. I reached out to Artemis again, with my whole heart, hoping my love could sustain us both.

We moved as quickly as we could, but the trail was narrow. Hunters pulled out their sickles and cut away parts of the path in front of me so I could walk beside the litter, but some places were just too narrow. When I let go the blood burst immediately from the wound, and Artemis woke, screaming. I would return my touch as quickly as possible, but each time we broke it, I became weaker and fainter. Apollo chewed bitter herbs and then pressed them to my lips to keep me moving. Others wiped my forehead and neck with cool water as we descended through the canopy of trees into the humid groves of mango, and I pressed on. I grew tired and weak, my eyelids heavy. An unquenchable thirst stripped my throat. Apollo made me chant. He called out the simplest words, and I repeated them to stay focused and awake. Still, several times I stumbled and fell, my knees and elbows bruised and cut. The wound on Artemis's leg sprang fresh with blood.

In the end, Coeus half carried me to the mouth of the trail and through the village. I was dimly aware of the crowd gathered around us, the surgeon's approach and then the sharp wail from Leto as we brought her daughter through the gates of their compound.

"Bring her here!" Leto commanded. She led us into the stone hall and closed the wooden doors behind us.

A bed had been prepared on the long table, and the room already smelled of boiling herbs and incense. Someone brought a chair for me. I almost collapsed in it. Apollo moved my hands away from Artemis's body and rubbed them. Another person pressed hot broth to my lips. The room was quiet except for the sound of Leto crying softly in Coeus's arms. Apollo spoke with the surgeon in a hushed voice.

I shut my eyes and rested as they moved me aside and examined Artemis's condition.

"I'm sorry," the surgeon said after a few minutes had passed.

I opened my eyes to see him shaking his head.

"It's too deep, and there's too much damage inside. She's lost too much blood. I can't even take the leg—"

"No," cried Leto moving to her daughter's side. "What can't be sewn with thread can be bound with the light!"

She turned to Apollo, but he shook his head.

"No," Leto whispered, "She is not meant to die like this."

Leto turned to me then. She pointed her finger and swooped around the table.

"Hera has already been able to stop the bleeding a great deal!" she said as if the answer was obvious.

She took hold of my wrist and pulled me back to Artemis, pushing the surgeon aside. She was a big woman, and strong, and the man stumbled to the floor. I dutifully put my hands back in their place. Apollo moved to her side and reached out to her gently.

"No, Mother," he said weakly. "Hera doesn't know enough to do something like this. She can't knit together the broken parts, just as the surgeon can't sew them. Hera can only stop the bleeding as long as she touches the leg."

Leto shook her head firmly.

"Don't let go," she said to me. "Don't let go of my girl."

She took her daughter's hand and pressed it to her cheek, letting out a soft moan.

"Don't let go," she said again. "Don't let go."

Coeus moved to her side. I heard his voice through a growing haze of heat in my head.

"We must not fear death, Leto," he said in a choked voice. "This is only a body. Artemis is immortal, like the true self of the animals we hunt. Now, we must let her body go."

"No," Leto said firmly. "There's another way."

"Mother, Hera can't keep this up," Apollo said. "No one can—"

"You're wrong. There's one person!" Leto's voice was fierce.

Despite my fatigue, my eyes flew open. Leto had pulled herself up. There was a command barely contained behind the flash of her eyes.

She turned to Coeus. "Send a boy to fetch Hera's mother!"

CHAPTER THREE

I stared at Leto in disbelief.

I'd grown up on the hill above the village where my parents lived an isolated life. Mother was a private woman. She didn't mingle in the market or buy beautiful things when the merchants passed through at festival time. Though she'd taught me the craft of herbs, I'd never seen her treat anyone other than Father and myself. I knew she had the gift of sight, but this wasn't something I'd ever told anyone—not even Artemis. Why Leto would call for Mother, I couldn't imagine.

A strong wave of anxiety overcame me. As it did, Artemis writhed on the table. Apollo looked up at me and shook his head sternly.

"You must stay calm, Hera," he said. Then more gently, "Just a little while longer."

My arms were heavy, and my head hurt. A sharp, jagged throbbing had seized my temples. I closed my eyes against it and became lightheaded. I felt my hands hot on Artemis's flesh, but the rest of my body seemed to be very far away.

Then Leto's big hands were on my forehead and a cool, wet cloth placed on my skin. She made me drink warm tea and pulled her shawl from around her shoulders and draped it over mine.

"You're doing well," she said in a familiar, soothing tone. "Stay with us, Hera."

Although my hands burned, a chill swept over my skin, and my teeth chattered. I felt faint. People gathered outside the door. A drumbeat had begun, and a chorus of song rose dimly about us. They chanted the sounds the healers used to pull flesh back together, but their voices were low and full of dread.

Then, I felt Mother's approach. I sensed her strength before she entered the room like a wave, easing the pounding in my head and the fear that had gripped me.

The drumbeat quickened as the door swung wide, and she stepped through, her tall, thin frame shrouded in her black cloak. Father was at her side. She didn't look at Leto or Coeus but fastened her eyes on mine as if she could hold me up with her gaze. I took in a sharp breath and felt the tears burning again on my cheeks. In a moment, she was across the room, and I felt her hands, cool on my face. She pulled my head against her body and stroked my hair gently. Something calm and soft seemed to move from her hands across my skin.

There was movement in the room, and I heard Leto's sharp cry as Father slid his arm around my waist and pulled me to my feet. My hands fell limp at my sides.

"No, no please!" Leto's voice was soft this time, pleading. "Hera stops the blood!"

Mother seemed not to hear her. She pulled deftly at the cord about her neck that was attached to a small vial of oil.

Struggling to keep my eyes open, I watched as she opened the vial, pouring a few drops into her open hand. The aroma was pungent at first so that I blinked and shook my head. A tingling sensation rippled down my limbs. Leto stepped back quickly, wiping at her eyes. In a moment the scent changed and a warm, intoxicating fragrance filled the room. Coeus placed his hands on Leto's shoulders to hold her steady as Mother poured the oil into her hand and anointed my forehead with it.

My eyelids fluttered, and I saw a flash of light followed by lovely warmth. For a moment I was weightless, without form and filled with peace. Eventually, my breath came easier, and I opened my eyes.

"Mother," I whispered. "I don't understand."

She shook her head. "You have opened too much, too fast," she answered. "It's dangerous for you, Hera. The oil will help your body regain its balance."

"What about Artemis," I began, "Somehow I'm helping her…" I couldn't finish as the fatigue overcame me again. I leaned heavily on father's shoulder.

Mother stared down at my friend's limp form. She reached out and took Artemis's wrist in her palm and shut her eyes. No one moved.

"There's nothing else you can do, Hera," Mother said quietly, laying Artemis's hand back down on the table. She looked around the room, and her eyes fell on Leto. "You have to let her go."

Artemis moaned, and I shuddered. Leto moved back to her daughter's side and took her hand. Artemis's eyes opened and closed, and she groaned in confusion.

"No," I said. "I was helping her. I could feel it, mother!" I tried to move toward Artemis, to raise my hands to her leg and take up my vigil, but Father held me fast.

"You've already done too much," his voice was firm. "She could take you with her when she goes."

Artemis cried out, low and bewildered as if reaching out when lost in the dark. My chest tightened.

"Then let her take me," I said pulling away from Father's grasp with my last bit of strength, laying my hands back on her leg.

Apollo, who had stood silently in the shadows, stepped to my side, laying his hands on mine. A long, quiet moment passed. The steady chanting outside was the only sound.

Then, I felt Mother come and stand beside me. She placed her hands gently on my shoulders and spoke to Father.

"There is only one way," she said.

Father's look was hard, but he nodded.

"Clear the room," he said to Coeus. "Everyone but the healers must go."

Coeus threw open the door and ordered everyone out. Leto looked up at Mother imploringly.

"Please let me stay. I'll tell no one what passes here, I swear it!"

Mother nodded. "But you must not let your grief interfere, Leto," she said.

When the room was empty of all the others, Mother poured the oil thickly into her hands and rubbed them together. Pulling away Artemis's tunic she pressed the oil onto her chest. Thick pieces of the ritual red clay shimmered on her breast as if coming alive, and the effect rippled across Artemis's skin and down her body. I watched, mesmerized, as Mother held her hands above Artemis's form, palms face down, moving slowly from her head to her feet. When she came to the torn leg, she didn't slow or stop, but the blood that had been seeping from the wound clotted.

Artemis lay in a deep, unconscious sleep. I looked down at her serene face, her cheeks filling again with color, and I let her go.

I shut my eyes then, letting my body finally collapse. There was a small commotion around me as my body was lifted. I was dimly aware of being carried, of the cool and moist air outside. At some point, I looked up at the sky and saw the stars spreading before me like a blanket of light.

They took me home and laid me on my bed. Someone covered me. Another pressed something bitter to my lips, and I drank it, letting its strong flavor lift me from my pain and exhaustion into a dream-like state.

Father whispered in my ear, "Let the herb take you, Hera. Have no fear of what you will see. You are initiated, my daughter, into the waking dream. When you return, your body will be restored." His voice was warm and familiar, but it began to fade as if he were speaking to me from far away.

"Have no fear, Hera," I heard him say. "Trust the waking dream."

Suddenly, I was in utter darkness, rushing up toward the sky, my body light and weightless and thin like air. I was aware of my surroundings, but couldn't feel any physical sensations or control the scenes.

Then I could see. I was outside in the night, moving through the sky. I saw the outline of our house and Father's taro fields just beyond, their long, wet rows shimmering in the full light of the moon. I laughed at the wonder of my movement. Stretching out beyond our land I saw the silver sea and the village lit with dim fires below me as I continued to rise.

I heard the sound of waves rolling onto the sand in the distance, and my long, black hair was loose, blowing behind me. I moved as if through soft, silken water. Up I rose, with a lightness of being, above my jungle home and over the side of the volcano. I had never been to the top, or to the other side of our island. There was a road leading there, but it took many days journey, and I'd never had a reason to go. The sea was the easiest way to move from one shore to another, but we lived so remotely that few ships ever came to our side. Now, as I rose above the land and sea, I perceived for the first time the immensity of our territory. As I passed over the volcano, I saw the sweeping expanse of Atlantis spread out before me, lit by the lovely, white glow of the moon and stars. Across the long valley I could make out the forested mountains to the north, and I could see the central city of Caledocean, luminous on the horizon. The tall pillars standing at its gates blazed with light even at this distance. I realized each pillar was crowned with a flame. I'd heard of this ritual—Caledocean's fires burning through the night—but I couldn't have imagined the grandeur of the site. I was dazzled and wanted to move toward them, but instead, I was pulled down to the west, over vast pastures and trees.

My movement slowed as I reached the shore where a small strip of beach and black rock sat beneath a gently sloping plateau. A great, yawning mouth of a cave was set back into the side of the hill, and just beyond I could make out the silhouettes of trees. A small fire crackled outside.

I couldn't feel my feet as I set down at the mouth of the cave, and yet somehow I stood before it. There was movement within, and for the first time, I felt anxiety move through my breast.

"Be calm, child," a woman's rough voice came from the cave.

I startled as an old woman walked forward from the darkness and into the light of the fire. She was slightly stooped, her skin black and coarse. Her hair hung in long, thick ringlets about her oval face. I tried to steady myself, but there was something peculiar about her form. Her tunic was simple, made of ordinary wool worn through in places and poorly patched. Her cape was no better, but the color was a vibrant scarlet that I'd never seen. She came and stood before me, her large, black eyes sharp as an owl's, looking me up and down.

I felt my breath become uneven and I tried to speak. "Who—"

"Be calm, girl," she said, her voice cracking as if it hadn't been used in a very long time. "So, you've finally found your power," she went on as if talking to herself. "And now you've come to me!"

Her eyes flashed in the firelight. I tried to step back, but my body wouldn't obey me. Again I felt afraid.

"You aren't in your physical body, child." Her voice was softer now. "But you're safe. I am a friend." She moved closer to me then and reached out as if she would touch me. As she did, I realized she wasn't solid either. She laughed.

"Yes, Hera," she said. "We dream this dream together! There is nothing to fear when you are with me. Come, I must show you something before your body calls you back."

She seemed to touch my hand, and to my delight, we lifted again toward the night sky. I laughed out loud at the dreamy sensation of flying, and she turned to me and smiled. Her face was a happy storm of creases.

I saw the city again, but we didn't head toward it. Instead, we turned inland and through the thick, green countryside, passing above large villages and towns with buildings and temples built in ways I'd never seen. Soon, we came to the edge of a vast lake. In the middle was an island, which looked as if it were floating in the mist and moonlight. I drew in my breath as I beheld it. "This is the Emerald Temple," she said. Her voice pulled me across the water and through the mist until we came to the isle.

I looked down at the buildings laid out around a large, circular structure capped by a massive dome. The roof was gilded, and it glittered in the moonlight. A large tree flowered at the base of a long, marble staircase at its entrance. There was a wonderful and intoxicating scent that washed over me as we approached.

"Here, the priestesses gather to control their minds and hone their skills."

I stared at the temple, rapt. There was something inside it, something alive that reached out to me and called my name. The night suddenly felt cool around me, as if my body were taking a more corporeal form.

The old woman made a sound of surprise.

"Remarkable," she said suddenly as if she'd noticed the change in me. "We must not linger so close to the temple," she finished.

We moved away from the holy place, over the gardens and outbuildings, to a very large and grand hall that sat on the top of a small incline overlooking the enclosure of buildings. We set down gently beneath the pillars of its portico, which stretched out for many lengths in both directions. The large wooden doors were thrown open to the warm, night air but the women that stood guard at the entrance didn't notice us at all. Torches burned in the wall beside them, and I saw short swords at their sides. I expected them to protest our presence, but the old woman only smiled and beckoned me to follow her inside.

We moved like ghosts through the inner hall, passing walls of frescoes, intricately carved statues and ornamented vases. The hallways were well lit with oil lamps. Somewhere close by I heard the sounds of people stirring, the familiar early morning rustling inside a kitchen. We continued past a large hall with rows of finely set tables until we came upon a broad marble staircase that spiraled to the floor above us.

The old woman touched me lightly, and we glided up it and then down a short corridor. I was enthralled by the scene, by how real everything appeared.

We came to a great wooden door with ornate dragons carved above it. Again, there was an armed woman stationed on either side. Neither seemed to see us, even when the old woman turned to me and whispered: "We're here."

She turned to the door before us and with a sudden, sweeping movement, pulled me through it. I gasped at the impossibility of the act, but in a moment we were standing in the room on the other side.

Silence.

I blinked in the dim candlelight that came from the alabaster altar in the center of the room. The flame shimmered off its surface as if it were dancing. Spices burned in a bowl at its center, and the room was filled with a potent scent of Frankincense and Myrrh that pulled me in.

Across from us stood a tall, heavyset woman looking out an arched window toward the lake. She stood very still, with a grave air about her. Her hair was unbound, like golden threads, and fell onto a rich ruby red robe of silk. We stood still, watching her for a moment, but then she turned sharply as if she were suddenly aware that we were there.

"Who is it?" she demanded, her voice firm and exact.

I was startled by her tone and the powerful step she took toward me.

"Who are *you?*" I quipped defensively. My voice was clear, and I was relieved to hear it.

"Who am I? Who am *I?*" A dark look crossed her face, and she raised herself up. "I am Rhea, High Priestess of the Emerald Temple." She took another step toward me, narrowing her eyes. "You will tell me your name at once, and you will kneel before me in respect, as is the custom here!"

Her voice was sharp, and I knew this was too real to be a dream. I wanted to take a step back, but I was frozen to the spot. Then I felt the old woman move out of the shadows and take a place beside me.

"It is *you* that shall kneel down, Rhea, before you will hear her name," she said.

The High Priestess was visibly startled, taking a step back toward the altar. Her face contorted in surprise and she inhaled sharply. She reached for a candle and held it high, her eyes growing wide as she recognized the old woman.

"Hecate?" she whispered.

The old woman laughed as the High Priestess took a step toward us, the light of the candle seeming to pass through my ethereal body. She stood a few feet away, her eyes large, blue pools of wonder.

"You travel in the Dreamtime," Rhea said, her voice low and with deference. "Forgive me, Hecate, Priestess of the Night."

She fell to her knees before us.

"The time has come," the old woman said. "Rhea, look upon the girl's face. Do you not recognize your own?"

Rhea stared up at me, and her look softened.

"Is it my Sofia, then?" she said sadly, holding up the light. "But you look so young, and it cannot be!"

"No, not Sofia," the old woman answered. "Look closer, and you will see the child's father in her eyes."

Rhea drew in her breath. "Sofia had a...*daughter?*" Her hand shook, casting shadows in frightening waves across the wall. "A daughter, an heir—"

"A queen," the old woman finished. Then she let out a wild cackle that pressed itself around my senses, and suddenly I was being pulled in a furious rush back over the water and up the mountain. All the while, the old woman's laughing voice was loud in my head like a drum beating a warning. I cried out, as one does in the face of inevitable unconsciousness, and then, everything was black.

CHAPTER FOUR

I SLEPT A LONG, DEEP, SLEEP, and when I awoke, I had only a vague sense of the dream. When I opened my eyes the windows were thrown open to the warm air, the sunlight bright in the room. I stirred slowly, testing the strength and authenticity of my limbs. My body was stiff. I felt Father's soft touch on my forehead.

"Be still, Hera. Your body is still recovering." His voice was filled with warmth and comfort.

I obeyed, relaxing my limbs into the soft mat beneath me. I lay there for a long time listening to the gentle sounds of the day. Small birds sang from the branches of the Lihue trees beneath the windows. The cries of the Cockatoos mounted as the sun flooded the room. Father sat beside me, his eyes half open, with a serene look that I was used to seeing. I smiled.

The small hearth was still glowing with embers, and a pot steamed warm above it. I could smell the brewing herbs.

"Mother?" My voice was coarse. When I swallowed, my mouth was dry and sore. Father lifted a cup, slid his hand behind my head, and helped me to raise myself. I sipped the tea.

"Mother and Artemis?" I asked again.

He patted my hand. "Your mother has repaired Artemis's leg. Now, they both must rest. Your mother rests in the temple and will join us in time."

He lifted the cup to my lips again, and I drank the rest of the herbs. Bitter though they were, they soothed my throat and strengthened my body. I moved my fingers, then my hands, lifting my arms from my side. As I did, scant images from my dream flashed in my mind as if pulling me toward them, but then they were gone.

"I was flying," I said softly, shutting my eyes, trying to remember. "Father, I was traveling through the sky—"

I opened my eyes to see him nodding.

"I had to give you a powerful herb," he said. "To relieve your body from the force it had been exerting. This set your true-self free to travel as it wished. I'm sorry I could not prepare you. What else do you remember?"

I shut my eyes and tried to go back to the dream, but everything was hazy and far away. A woman, a strange, holy place and the dragons carved on the door. I told him these things. He nodded and urged me to go on, but the rest was vague.

"It may come back in time," he said. "And you may have…questions. Come to me if you recall more. Now, let us see if you are strong enough to rise."

He slipped his arm around me, helping me to my feet. As I stood, I saw that I wore the same tunic stained with blood, earth, and sweat.

"Please take me to the pool so I may bathe."

Just below our home, we had dammed the stream, making a small, freshwater pool. Father took me there, sliced open a red awapuhi plant to soap myself with, and left me there to wash.

I pulled the linen tunic off and stepped into the water. Cold rippled up and over my skin. I eased my body into the deepest part of the pool, submerging my head. My hair fanned out, weightless above me, and when I came up for air, I let it cling to my cheek, neck, and breasts. I took the awapuhi plant and squeezed the juice into my hands, covering my body with it. The sweet floral scent of ginger rose from the liquid, and I smoothed the next handful through my hair, washing away the hardship that still clung to me. I let myself rest then, in the cool of the stream's peaceful rhythm, knowing those I loved were safe.

When I emerged from the pool, I lay naked in the sun, letting my skin dry. Then I wrapped the thin cloth of my pareo around my waist and crossed it over my breasts. It tied behind my neck.

I returned to the house where Father had set the table outside. We ate in silence. I sliced the fresh breadfruit and papaya, scooping the seeds out with my fingers. Each mouthful gave me strength, pushing away the sense of timelessness and unreality of the night before so that soon, I thought of my bodiless journey as a dream. The past day's hunt and the grueling hours that followed felt far away.

I rested all afternoon while Father went to his fields. When he returned, I boiled the taro and served him. He disappeared after the meal to tend Mother who still retreated in his temple on the hill. That night, as I lay down to sleep, I caught a glimpse of the starry sky through the smoke hole in the top of our roof and shivered. I felt momentarily weightless, and the determined blue eyes of the woman from my dream flashed before me. I tried to picture her, to remember the words she had said, but they eluded me, as fatigue took my body, and I fell asleep.

The next day I went with Father to the fields. Beside him, in the knee-deep water, we pulled up the arrow-shaped leaves and collected the roots. When the sun was high above us, he gave me leave, and I headed for the path that led down to the village. I wanted to see Artemis. I picked fresh lilikoi for Leto on the way, concerned about how she would receive me. In the past, she had treated me as one of her own, but now that my recklessness had caused her such pain, I wasn't sure what to expect.

I pulled up the hem of my tunic to carry the fruit, feeling calm and sweet, humming to myself as I went. When I reached the bottom of the trail, I moved toward the beach, passing the fishermen pulling their outriggers onto the shore. They had made a tremendous catch, hauling in nets filled with fish. I stopped a moment to watch.

The men wore loincloths, their chests bare, as they worked. Their dark, muscled chests, were covered with blue symbols some that wound about their arms in elaborate patterns.

One of the young men looked up from his work and saw me. He stopped and raised his hand above his head. It was Ano, a young man I'd often tried to get to know, but he had never paid any attention to me. He called out my name, waving his hand vigorously, and began to move toward me. I raised my hand in reply and smiled not sure what to do. He called my name again, and this time, the other fishermen, young and old, dropped their nets pointing in my direction. A group of them hastened toward me with baskets and a giant fish. Ano led the way.

"Hera," Ano said as they reached me.

"She is Lady Hera, now," an older man said.

I looked at him in surprise, but before I could respond another man handed me a basket. Ano took a large piece of fish and wrapped it in taro leaves, laying it inside.

"The biggest fish carries the greatest life force," the eldest man said, "It will give you strength, Lady."

I stood, speechless. His tone held deference and respect. I knew I couldn't refuse their kindness without offending them, so I took the basket, dropping the fruit I kept in my hem as I did. Ano scrambled to pick the lilikoi up, placing them in the basket beside the fish as if they were precious things.

"Its good to see you, Lady Hera," he said, his smiling almost too big for his face.

"Thank you," I stammered, and then turning to the rest of the men, "Thank you!"

I backed away awkwardly, returning to the path and walked toward the village. Moving quickly, I passed by the huts on the beach and into the marketplace, unnerved. As I walked through the open stalls, I hardly noticed the new fabrics and tapa cloths laid out for show. Suddenly a sharp wind blew through the market, and a rare streak of ruby red silk blew loose from its line wrapping itself about me. I sucked in my breath, a sharp flash of memory from my dream rising before me. An image of the blond haired woman in a ruby red robe... but the remembrance faded.

"Take it, Lady!" It was the voice of old Helene standing beside me. "It would be my honor for you to have it!"

I turned abruptly to see her stooped form and toothless grin. She reached up adjusting the cloth around my shoulders.

"Yes, yes," she said, "this is the color of the Sacred Feminine. You must have it!"

People had gathered around and were nodding assent.

"It's a royal color," one of them said approvingly.

"And real silk, brought from Caledocean," another added with obvious delight.

I shook my head, confused. I had nothing to trade for it, and no coin. Never had I worn such a thing of finery, and never had I considered that anyone cared if I would. I refused again, but Helene pushed the cloth into my free hand.

"A gift, Lady," she said, patting my hand and then stepped back into the gathering crowd.

A woman beside her reached out and put a small item wrapped in *tapa* into my basket.

"For your mother," she said.

There were nods of assent all around me, and others pushed forward, laying gifts in my basket. I tried to smile as I backed away, but even as I retreated they laid their finery upon me—a strand of pearls, a pumice bowl, fresh coconut meat and a small conch shell, polished so that my dark eyes flashed across the surface.

"Please," I stammered, "I don't know—"

"There's nothing to say," Helene's voice cut across my own. "We ask only for your blessing," she said.

The words rang out and silenced the crowd. My body shook slightly. I stood blankly for another moment, then nodded and forced a smile, before quickly turning toward the path to Leto's house.

As I passed beyond the lava rock walls and the outer buildings, several of the men who were roasting meat over the fire turned to watch me pass. I stepped more quickly. Leto's women who chatted at the looms beneath the palms grew silent as I slipped by. To my shock, they dropped their heads slightly as I passed.

I gripped the basket then and broke into a run through

the courtyard to the long, narrow cookhouse where I knew I would find Leto. Artemis, if she was recovered enough, was sure to be in her company. As I rounded the bamboo patch, running much too fast with my heavy load, I stumbled and fell. Strong hands reached around my waist and steadied me. I spun around to see Apollo grinning.

"Hera," he began, but something stopped him, perhaps the look on my face.

He reached out and took the basket from my hands, keeping his arm tight about me as I leaned on him for support. He called out for his mother, and in a moment Leto was there, her big hand wrapped around my arm, pulling me inside. She gave me water and pushed a bowl of steaming meat toward me. I shook my head.

"I'm alright," I said feeling foolish. "It's just that people are acting so strangely." I pointed at the basket overflowing with gifts and held out the crimson silk. Leto nodded, as if in satisfaction.

"Signs of respect," she said, taking the silk in her hands and holding it up to the light. "Very fine indeed." She folded it up carefully and placed it over the conch in the basket.

"But respect of what?" I asked. "Everything was my fault in the first place if it wasn't for me —"

"No, child, none of that," Leto said sternly. "Artemis is going to be alright, and that's what matters. The accident was a hardship that served a profound purpose to you and the people of our village. It revealed so much about you. We've always known mistress Tethys and your father, Oceanus, were—" she hesitated, *"different.* Your parents came to us from the other side of the island and kept to themselves and their spiritual traditions. They never learned our ways. But you, Hera, were born here, and I dare say you've spent as much time with my family as you have with your own. You're one of us, do you understand?"

I smiled awkwardly. "I think so."

She pointed again to the basket of offerings. "Accept the gifts with grace, child. You belong to this village. Your honor is their honor! There is a reason all of this happened. We just don't know what it is yet."

Apollo nodded, adding, "The reason will reveal itself in its time."

Leto turned to the door and urged me to my feet.

"Artemis is in the garden," she said, her tone endearing.

I glanced at Apollo who sat fingering the silk. As I stepped out the door, I caught his words spoken in a low tone to his mother. "It's the High Priestess's color," he said.

I found Artemis sitting beneath a banyan with her legs stretched out before her on a thick mat. She smiled when she saw me coming. I kneeled beside her. She reached her arms out to me, slipped them around my neck and brushed my cheek with her lips. I looked into her eyes, searching for blame or regret, but found only the ancient, black stillness that I was used to.

She pulled up the sarong that covered her injured leg, pressing my finger to the thick scar that ran down to the knee. The skin was slightly raised, but the wound looked like it had been healing for months, not days. I shook my head in amazement.

"It's not even tender," she said, and let go of my hand. "It only hurts when I walk, and your mother says that will go away in time. She is a powerful Scent Priestess, Hera."

"A Scent Priestess?" I questioned.

"A healer," Artemis replied. "One who can merge with the vibration of plants, and draw out their sacred medicine. Every temple dedicated to the Mother has a Scent Priestess within it. She is the anointer, the healer, and the guide through birth and death. It is a deeply honored role, Hera."

"My mother, a Scent Priestess," I said slowly. "But where did she learn such a thing? Why didn't she tell me?"

Artemis shook her head.

"I think she will have to tell you now," she said. "Things are going to be different now that your own skills as a healer have emerged."

I didn't know what to say. I rocked back on my feet, sitting down beside her, and dropped my head onto her shoulder as I often did. I shut my eyes.

Artemis lifted my hand to her lips. "Thank you," she said in a soft voice.

I smiled. She squeezed my hand, letting it rest on her lap.

A breeze moved through the leaves above us, and the sun was warm on my skin. Listening to her breath, I felt my body soften. The scent of coconut oil rose from her body, and a wisp of her thick, black hair brushed against my lips sending a pleasurable sensation down my spine.

I opened my eyes and looked up into her face. Her eyes were half closed and her mouth slightly open. I felt her breath move against me, and I opened my mouth as if to take it in. My mind flashed to the ritual before the hunt, the full, chiseled features of her face transforming before me, the animal nature in her bones rising to touch the animal within me.

I leaned forward, pressing my lips to hers. Heat flooded my skin, and I wanted something more. I turned my body and moved toward her, but Artemis put her hands on my shoulders. She pushed me away, gently.

I caught my breath, opening my eyes. She shook her head.

"No, dearest, we can't," she said softly.

"Why?" I demanded. "You've always been with women, why not me?"

"Hera," Artemis began, but she hesitated.

"You're not attracted to me," I said flatly as if my world had dissolved.

She raised her brow and laughed, "No, that's not it," she said. "You are so beautiful, Hera."

I softened. "Then why?"

She reached her hand out to my cheek affectionately but frowned.

"Hera, you're my friend, not my lover. You're young, and you have so many pleasures to explore."

I nodded eagerly, "Yes," I replied, "So many pleasures and I want to explore them with *you.*"

She shook her head again. "That would change things between us, Hera."

"But something's already changed!" I insisted. "The hunt, the boar, and the heat in my body—" I struggled to find the words.

She reached out again and took my hand, pulling it to her chest.

"Hera, I intend to be your friend always, no," she held up her hand as I began to protest. "Listen to me, try to understand. You will enjoy the company of women, I see that, but you will also enjoy the company of men. You must remain free in your heart to do so. You have a long life ahead of you."

An odd chill swept over my flesh as she said these words. My body shivered.

I looked into her eyes letting go of the disappointment

and hurt that were arising. After a long moment, I spoke the only true thing I knew.

"I love you, Artemis."

"I know," she said. "And I love you, Hera."

She pulled me toward her so that I took my place beside her again. I leaned in close and shut my eyes. She wrapped her arm around me. The breeze arose, gentle and warm, carrying with it the sweet scent of plumeria. I breathed it in, and my heart quieted.

"There is one more thing, my friend," Artemis said, her voice very warm and low. "You saved my life, and one day, I know I will do the same for you."

That odd sensation and chill swept over me again.

We sat in silence as the afternoon faded to dusk.

When the women put aside their weaving and came outside, stretching their backs and hooting at the reddening sky, I stood and helped Artemis to her feet. She moved slowly, limping, leaning on my shoulder as we moved toward the weavers. As we neared them, a silence fell over the group, until Leto approached and wrapped me in her arms. I disappeared in her soft flesh.

The other women surrounded me then, patting my back affectionately, stroking my head in praise. We all strolled out to the beach together. We took up hands, turned to the sky, and watched the sun set into the sea.

CHAPTER FIVE

I DIDN'T SEE MOTHER UNTIL DUSK of the next day. She stood at the top of the path waving to Father and me as we made our way back from the field. She was tall and wore her hair in a long black braid down her back. Beautiful streaks of silver were woven throughout. Her skin was very white, much paler than my own, and so she wore a thin linen gown with long sleeves to protect it. I had her full lips and round face, but not her eyes. My eyes were shaped more like my father's, angled and deep-set, while Mother's eyes were soft and shockingly blue.

I ran up the path to greet her. I flung myself happily into her open arms, as she laughed out loud, squeezing me tight. Then she kissed both my cheeks and held me at arm's length, just looking at me.

"I'm fine," I tried to reassure her, but as I spoke, I noticed the dark hollows beneath her own eyes.

"Mother, are you alright?"

"I am, sweet girl," she said.

She released me, turning to Father, who put an arm around her and moved toward the house. I took the tools from his other hand to bring them to the shed, but I stopped midway. Turning back I watched my parents walk together in a slow, graceful rhythm. There was something in their manner that spoke to me of swans. I'd seen the magnificent white birds once. They had landed in the freshwater pool by the village. Someone had said they'd come all the way from the other side of the island where the great lake was their home. I'd watched them in wonder as they glided across the surface of the water as if it were empty space, their necks brushing gently one against the other.

As they reached the doorway, my parents stopped and turned to see me staring. Mother waved again, and then they turned and went in.

I hurried through my chores and then came inside. The room was long and thin. Mother had already lit the fire that was set in a stone pit in the middle, and a slim line of smoke moved up toward the hole in the center of the arched roof. On one side stood a table made from a thick piece of dark Koa wood. Father had made it and the benches positioned at either side. Across the room lay my parents' sleeping mat and their wooden chests, intricately carved and gilded. A thin, wooden panel slid open and closed just beyond, separating my room from the rest. Shelves lined the tall walls by the hearth, full with Mother's little pots of herbs and spices, and the gourds of her thick honey. In summer, when we harvested from the hives, the room always smelled of honey and wax. Candles hung in long, clumped forms from the shelves where we'd left them to harden.

I stoked the fire and set the water pot to boiling, then pulled bread from the basket and sliced it thickly onto our bamboo plates. As I boiled the taro and greens, I watched

Father press firmly on different points on Mother's hands, massaging them in small, circular motions. He moved up her arms and to her shoulders until she sighed and shut her eyes. She rested there quietly while I brought our supper to the table.

Father took a timber from the fire and lit the candles. Mother reached for the serving spoon. There was an effort in her movement as if her arms had lost their strength.

"Here, Mother," I said, "let me serve you tonight."

She cocked her brow but sat back. Father reached for her hand.

"Tethys, you need more rest," he said.

She nodded. "It's been so long since I've used such a force."

I wanted to know more, to ask what she meant and how she'd managed to heal Artemis, but my father gave me a stern look.

"More rest," he said again as much to me as to Mother.

"It's alright, Oceanus," Mother said as I filled her plate and sat back down. "The healing ability doesn't always take its toll in such a way, Hera. But Artemis was close to death, and I went beyond healing to bring her back. This won't happen to you after you have been trained."

I turned to her excitedly. "You're going to teach me?"

Father frowned. "Just enough to control it, so you won't get hurt," he said.

I looked down at my plate, feeling discouraged.

"But how is it that you can heal, Mother?" I avoided Father's gaze.

There was a silence so long that I looked up from my food. Father's face looked strained, and Mother seemed to be looking to him as if he would answer for her. He only sat there and the moment dragged on, uncomfortably.

"What is it?" I asked, this time looking directly at Mother. "How do you know to heal this way?"

She reached out to me across the table, her hand trembling slightly as she closed it around my own. Leaning toward me, she spoke in a quiet voice.

"The ability runs in my family, Hera." She stopped there, and I could feel the heat of Father's gaze on us both.

"Just because you have a mystic gift does not mean it has to be your life, Hera," Father said. "I want you to be happy. I want so very much for you to be free."

"Free?" I said annoyed. "If it were up to you I'd never leave this land!"

Both my parents stopped eating and stared at me.

"I'm sorry," I said moving the food from one side of my dish to the other. "It's just that things are different now. I'm different! And I want to know what I can do, what I can *really* do."

There was a long, uncomfortable silence, but I did not look up or retract my words. I'd had enough of this place and my parent's solitude.

"Your gifts will lead you to a very different sort of life with people who will change you," Father finally said.

I looked up then and stared him in the eye with defiance. "And what's wrong with that?" Turning to my mother, I demanded, "How do you know how to heal? Who trained you?"

"My mother trained me," she said. "And life of course, in the way only life can." She let out a heavy sigh. "When I have regained my strength I will begin your training," she said.

I moved from my chair and hugged her. "Thank you!" I said. "Thank you."

She embraced me, but when I sat back down the look on her face was regretful and sad.

I turned to my father, but he slid from the bench and left the house without a word.

The days that followed were long and slow. I stayed with Mother as she regained her strength doing my best to curb my desire to learn more.

Then, one late afternoon I slipped out to see Artemis. As I moved through the village, I was surprised at how quickly I had grown accustomed to the way people had changed their manner toward me. I strode with a cat's grace, wearing my hair long down my back and pressing fresh ginger to my skin before I went. I wore the string of pearls. Mother gave me honey, soft in the pots, to bring to Leto and her women, and this brought the bees to me. As I walked through the village, they danced in small formations of orange and gold about me. While I was used to them and they to me, others gave me a full berth, which let me pass with little more than admiring looks.

When I came to old Helene's, she swiped at the bees with her hand. "Your mother?" she asked. "Is the Lady Tethys up and about?"

I nodded, veering away from her as the bees hummed with agitation.

"Yes, all is well," I said quickly, avoiding her flapping hands, continuing on my way.

The next morning as I prepared to leave for the field I heard a voice calling from outside, "Hello, hello!"

Father looked up from his tea, startled. No one ever ventured past the village and up our hill. He got quickly to his feet, and I followed him outside where, to my surprise, old Helene was making her way, unabashedly, toward us. She waved her hand above her head as if she were an old friend of Father's. I recognized her two granddaughters following close behind her. One was Callidora, dark-skinned and round with child. The other was a girl I knew from the hunt, Desma, very fair and slight. She smiled at me apologetically as her grandmother bustled up to us.

Father stood still beside me as they approached, but I could sense his distress. He did not raise his arms in welcome. For a moment, I felt awkward not knowing how to greet them until I heard Mother's voice from the door.

"Blessed be, Helene," she said, moving quickly past my father's rigid form with her arms held out in a gesture of greeting. Reluctantly, Father followed, repeating her gesture to the girls. Helene didn't reach for Mother's hands. "Lady," she said, bobbing her head.

Father stiffened. Mother tried to calm him with a gentle touch on his arm, but his voice came out harshly. "Hera," he said, "we'll be late to the fields."

He turned to leave. Reluctantly, I turned away to follow him, but Mother placed her hand on my shoulder.

"I'll need Hera with me today," she said.

He stopped and faced her, a dim tension between them. I looked at Father but felt Mother's hand firm on my shoulder. He narrowed his eyes disapprovingly, but said nothing, turning toward the fields.

Helene seemed not to notice the exchange. She gestured at Callidora's belly, beckoning the woman to her side and listed all of the girl's woes to Mother. She explained the painful pregnancy, the long, sleepless nights, and how difficult it was to keep anything down, even at this late stage. Mother listened intently, nodding reassurance. Callidora looked at Mother with hope in her eyes, and I realized they had come here for healing. My body thrilled.

Gesturing toward the house, Mother led us inside, and we took up seats about the table. Mother took hold of Callidora's wrists. I knew she was feeling the pulses, as she'd done this to me many times before when I was ill. From the beat and its rhythm, she would prescribe the herbs or scented oils she'd use to make Callidora well.

I watched her carefully, how she touched Callidora, and listened to the kind of questions she asked. Was there heat in her legs? Did her headache? Was her tongue on fire? She bade me grind the herbs and then sprinkled chamomile flowers into a pot with them, letting them boil, all the while nodding amicably as Helene talked on and on about her children.

"I've ten of them, you know," she said with pride. "A long life and ten healthy babes." She shook her head and put a wrinkled hand to her cheek. "All girls!"

Mother poured Callidora a cup of tea and put the rest in a large gourd for her to take with her. I stretched my back. They'd been with us for a long time, and I could see Mother growing tired as well. The window cloths were pulled aside, and the air circulated freely through the door, yet the house was warm from the hot stones around the fire. The air smelled of the potent, bitter herbs we'd been brewing. I wiped the perspiration from my forehead with the back of my hand. Desma noticed and picked up the gourd from the table ready to leave, but her grandmother didn't move.

"Not that I mind having all girls, what a blessing, what a blessing—"

I was growing irritated. They'd received what they'd come for, and now Mother needed to rest. I opened my mouth to say so, but Mother caught my eye and shook her head. She reached for a chair and pulled it up next to old Helene, and took the aged hand in her own.

"Is there anything else I can do for you?" she asked kindly.

Helene quieted. Then she leaned closer, dropping her voice low as if she shared a secret.

"My mate has no namesake," she said.

Her voice was sad, and for the first time, Helene seemed frail to me. Mother nodded thoughtfully, but her eyes were dark and unreadable disks.

"All girls, you see," Helene went on. "I love my girls, but if this baby were a boy—"

Again Mother nodded, but this time she turned to Callidora.

"I can catch the babe's sex if you wish," she said.

The young woman was surprised, but Helene's face broke into a grin, her wrinkles bringing her more to life.

"Yes, yes, I knew she could do it, her kind always can!" she said to her granddaughter. "You're too young to re-member. But there was a time when all women could do such things."

"But how?" Callidora asked.

"Everything is made of the same life force," Mother ex-plained, but she was looking at me. "Imagine it as an invis-ible current that is both formlessness and form. Though we have *visible* bodies, we also exist as this *invisible* current. We are…both."

She stopped for a moment. I could hear the lazy sound of her bees outside the window, and the breeze rustling through the gardenia. We all leaned forward waiting for her to speak. She dropped her eyes from mine and turned again to Callidora.

"The most important thing to understand is that everything is made from this invisible force. And when we touch the invisible, formless self we can have as much effect on the body as when we touch the visible form. You just need to know how."

The young woman blinked. She put her hand on her belly. Intrigue flashed in her eyes. "So, you can contact the child?" she said. "You know how to speak with the life force?"

Mother nodded and smiled.

Callidora smiled back. "Please, tell me what you can!"

I watched carefully as Mother placed her hand over Callidora's own and shut her eyes.

"I gently rest," she said in a soft, musical tone, "into the invisible current—"

My body relaxed, and my hands grew warm as she spoke. I sensed a sinuous heat pulsing through my limbs. My cheeks grew warm, my lips dry, and I felt a sense of peace. Mother went on.

"This current contacts itself within you in the form of the child. In this way, for a moment," she hesitated, taking another deep breath, "we are one."

Callidora's cheeks flushed, and she closed her eyes. She swayed slightly as if this invisible current Mother spoke of had swept her up into it. She smiled broadly. I felt my own eyes growing heavy, and my body also swayed. *Soft. Rose. Girl.* These words crossed my mind. My body still swayed. Desma, who sat next to me, swayed as well. She brushed up against my arm, gently, and the thoughts changed. *Warm. Willing. Boy.* I opened my eyes and turned to my friend, but she was still mesmerized by the sound of Mother's voice.

"Everyone can perceive the current, to become one with it and live their life from this unified perspective," Mother finished, lifting her hands from Callidora's.

She sat back in her chair with a look of serenity in her eyes.

"You will be graced with a daughter," she announced. "Blessed be."

Callidora looked relieved, and tears came to her eyes. She leaned forward to take Mother's hands, kissing them with gratitude. Then, she seemed to remember her grandmother who sat dejectedly beside her, shaking her head.

Callidora forgot her joy and hung her head apologetically. I felt terrible for her. Helene stood slowly, reaching for her other granddaughter's arm. Desma took the old woman's hand dutifully.

"It's not that I don't love my girls," she said again turning away from Callidora, "But a boy before I'm gone—"

"There will be other children," Callidora ventured.

Helene shook her head.

"I'm too old to wait," she said. Callidora visibly sagged beneath her words. "This was my last hope."

I was growing vexed. "You should be happy for Callidora," I said roughly, but as soon as I said it, I had regret for Helene looked suddenly old and vulnerable once again.

She looked up at me, wringing her hands in a feeble gesture as if she was worried that she'd upset me. "It will be alright," I assured her.

Still, she reached out and snatched my hands. Her eyes narrowed, and her cheeks grew very pale.

"I didn't mean to offend," she said her voice shaking. "I love my girls, all my girls," she said frantically.

Callidora moved to her grandmother's side, trying to calm her, but the old woman had tears in her eyes. Mother gave me a reproachful look.

My discomfort grew.

"I'm sorry," I said, "It's just that you shouldn't give up hope. There's always Desma's baby," I offered hopefully.

Desma turned toward me sharply. Her face grew pale.

"Desma has been promised to the temple, she's still untouched," Helene began through her tears, but seeing the look on her granddaughter's face, she stopped.

She looked from the girl to me.

"Grandmother," Desma stammered, "grandmother, I—"

Helene's eyes grew wide. My mother was on her feet now and at my side.

"But no one knows—" Desma said falteringly. "No one knows yet, not even—" She stopped abruptly, glaring at me.

There was an awkward moment of silence, and then Mother took Desma firmly by the elbow, cooing reassurances and blessings as she moved her toward the door. Callidora put her arm through Helene's, who still stood wide-eyed and speechless, and followed. When I tried to follow them, Mother gestured for me to stay. I watched helplessly as they disappeared behind the *tapa* cloth that fell shut behind them.

I waited a long time listening to their raised voices and Mother's soothing tone. Anxiously, I cleaned up the tea and herbs until all was in its place. Still, Mother didn't return. I sat down helplessly and buried my head in my hands. Why had I been so short with Helene? And how had I known about the baby?

When Mother returned she looked exhausted and weak, and yet her eyes seemed calm.

"I see you have much to learn," she said, her voice filled with amusement.

I was startled. "You're not angry with me?"

She shook her head. "Your ability is extraordinarily

strong, Hera. I didn't realize. The fault was my own."

"But old Helene—"

"You've only made her more in awe of you," she said grinning. "We'll be lucky if she doesn't bring every single girl from the village to you for visioning!"

I put my hand over my mouth, but we laughed together. She sat down again in the chair by the window and shut her eyes as the sun warmed her face. I sensed her resting again, as she had done with Callidora, only this time she seemed to be merging with the yellow rays of light.

"Mother," I said softly, "One day, will I have the gift of healing the way you do?"

She didn't open her eyes. "You have it already, Hera. In time, I will teach you to harness it so that you may use it without harm to yourself."

"And will people respect me for my gift, mother?"

Still, her eyes were closed. The sunlight intensified, casting a golden hue the length of her unbound hair. When she spoke, her voice sounded sad.

"When you step fully into your own gift, Hera." she said, "They will bow down before you."

CHAPTER SIX

A FULL SEASON PASSED.

I had stopped going to the fields with Father because Mother and I had been seeing a steady flow of people for healing. Helene had fulfilled Mother's prediction, bringing more than just pregnant girls to our door. As the weeks passed, more and more of the sick arrived, forcing me to learn my new trade quickly. There were many new faces and people from villages with names I'd never heard of. I reveled in the activity of my new life.

Mother put Helene in charge of collecting more herbs, and the old woman took to the task with zeal, sending her daughters out with collections of leaves to categorize and gather. Then she organized builders from the village to erect a drying room below our home. Even Father seemed to settle into the new routine, nodding to old Helene each morning, as he went alone to tend his fields.

For the first time I began to feel that I had a purpose, and as Mother helped me awaken my gift of healing I found myself feeling stronger and growing happier. My life fell into a gentle and pleasing rhythm, until the day the soldier came to our door for healing.

He arrived early one morning, pacing outside our door as the sun began to rise. Father was annoyed.

"We haven't even taken our morning meal," he said, frowning.

Mother went to the door and signaled the young man to come in. He walked with a jagged gait. Once inside he rocked back and forth. His eyes narrowed as he looked about the room, then he averted his gaze. Father stopped frowning and offered him a chair. Usually, he would've taken his pack and headed out early, leaving us to the healing work, but I felt his concern at the young man's presence.

"What's your name?" Father asked.

"Anthros, sir, I'm a soldier with the ninth legion stationed in the tribal lands of Ur—" He faltered. "I *was* a soldier," he amended.

Mother brought food to the table with a plate for Anthros. He bent his head.

"Thank you, Lady," he said, his eyes averted. He continued to rock even in his seat.

I sat down beside him as Mother brewed his tea. He looked very young to be a soldier and younger still to have taken part in a journey across the world to Ur, yet his face was earnest as he spoke, and the thick scar along his cheek proved more then he could say.

"And now you've returned to Atlantis," Father pressed. "Where are you from?"

"I've come from Caledocean," Anthros answered. "My uncle lives just a short way from here, and he came to fetch me for your healing."

Father's mouth opened as if to speak, but then he closed it and said nothing. His forehead creased. Mother seemed surprised as well.

"That's a very long way to come," she said weakly. "I hope I can help you."

"They say you've got quite the gift, and that you can heal what can't be seen."

"*They* say—" Father repeated. "Are you saying that they've heard of her in Caledocean?" His voice was clearly strained as if struggling with his temper. I looked at Mother, but even she seemed upset.

"I've been to the temple there, but the priests can't help me, they can't—" again his words dropped off, and he shook his head. "They can't see what ails me."

Mother recovered herself and reached out a kind hand directing Anthros to eat. He did as she directed. His hand shook slightly as he lifted the drink to his lips.

Father rose and left the room. Mother's eyes followed him as he went, but she stayed by the soldier's side as he ate. She asked him mild questions about himself, his family and friends. I sensed her approaching the reason for this visit in a roundabout way.

Anthros ate the food on his plate, and I cleared it. Mother pulled down a jug, far back on a shelf, and poured him some wine. This was unusual. She filled his mug without watering it down and bade him drink. Again, he did just as she said. The wine didn't take long to relax the man, and soon he spoke more freely.

"—and then you sailed to Ur," Mother urged him forward in his story.

"Yes. We sailed past the great pillars and deep into the Aegean until we met the rebellious tribes. Then—" I felt the pain well up in him, "I haven't been right since."

"But why were you there?" I asked, "Why were you making war on the tribes?"

Mother shook her head to silence me, and I realized my mistake, but it was too late. I'd pushed him toward the wound too fast. His eyes seemed to glaze, and his hand shook much harder than before. His rocking became more severe. He didn't answer me, just shook his head and mumbled,

"Why? Why?"

I felt the healing heat move from Mother's body toward him and then she leaned over, stroking his head as if he were a part of her in some way.

"Anthros," she began, "faced the fury of the tribes to procure more land for Atlanteans."

He continued to shake, shudder and mumble.

Mother spoke, "It has long been rumored that Olympia may one day erupt again. If it should our leaders think it prudent to have other settlements established."

I'd heard the story before, but Mother seemed to be saying it more for the soldier than for me. As she said it, Anthros seemed to come to himself. He looked fervently into Mother's eyes.

"Is there not land enough for all?" he said, clenching the breast of his tunic. "Why must we kill to take their land? If they were there first, shouldn't we let them be?"

"That would be one choice," Mother said, her voice taking on a soothing, hypnotic tone I'd come to recognize as the beginning of her healing grace. Then she came to sit beside him. She touched him very lightly on the shoulder. "Who did you hurt, Anthros? Who haunts you?"

The young man looked wild-eyed now, rocking, and rocking.

"There were children," he said. "There were women in their beds—"

He wept then, and Mother put her soft hands on his head as he curled in on himself, the heat of her gift moving over him in waves. We sat there with him a very long time until he quieted and stilled. She shut her eyes, and I knew she was soothing something much deeper than a physical wound.

Soon, his movements slowed, and his breathing returned to normal. There was a deep sigh as he straightened himself, wiping at his eyes and cheeks with the hem of his garment. He seemed dazed.

When Mother opened her eyes, they were filled with tears.

After some time, I heard movement outside and stepped out to find Helene and two of her daughters laying baskets of fresh herbs on the table, in the sun. Others were arriving behind them for healings. When I returned to the house, Mother had Anthros on his feet and helped guide him out of the house to a mat in the shade of the Lihue tree beyond the herb shed. Mother kneeled and covered him with a blanket.

"Rest now, Anthros. Sleep if you can," she said. "Let your body grieve. Let it tremble and release what has been done."

She anointed him with oils and held his hand for a while longer, and then tenderly as if he was her own son, she leaned over him and kissed his forehead.

"You can not change the past," she whispered. "You must make peace with it and move on and do something good with your life."

Tears rolled down Anthros's cheeks.

"Yes, Lady," he said, shutting his eyes.

His body shook gently, and Mother seemed pleased. After a while longer it stopped, and he drifted to sleep. Mother stood.

"Blessed be," she said.

We tended to the sick throughout the afternoon, but Mother was distracted. When finally she could return to the soldier, he was gone. A pile of plumeria blossoms was laid down in his place. Mother explained it was an ancient custom, a deeply honored offering of thanks. I tried to ask her more about him, more about this war but she shook her head and spread her hands over her eyes.

"This expansion has hurt so many," she muttered. "Unnecessary deaths, unnecessary suffering...I must help when I can."

She seemed pained by the subject, so I let it go.

At dusk, Father came up the path, but he wasn't alone. He led a brindled mare with short legs and a beautiful mane behind him. We had goats for milk and cheese but had never had need of a horse before.

"Is she for riding?" I asked excitedly, reaching out my hand to brush her soft nose.

She moved forward, nuzzling me.

"If need be," he said. "But her usual work is to carry things. We may need her in the times to come."

Mother gave him a pained look but said nothing.

I took the mare and tethered her on a long stretch of rope at the edge of the field where the grass was high, but where she could still reach the stream to drink. She was gentle and easy, but I knew little of horses and their ways. I would have Artemis show me how to ride.

When I returned to the house, it was dark outside, and the sky curved, blue-black and fringed with silver stars. I stopped outside the door to watch the last bit of light escape when I heard my parents' raised voices.

"She's too young, Tethys, and too untamed. She won't understand!"

Mother's voice was low as she replied. I stepped quickly to the window, sinking down to my knees, straining to hear.

"No," it was Father again. "We don't have time to wait. Word is spreading."

The horse whinnied loudly and then stopped. I heard footsteps as Mother moved toward the window and I slunk away.

When I entered the house they were quiet, Father carving his wooden animals in the far corner, and Mother in her chair before the red embers that glowed inside the circle of stones. There was a slight tension between them that was new to me.

I felt uneasy. I slid down to the ground beside Mother, laying my head against her knee. She reached out to stroke my hair and softly hummed a familiar tune from my childhood. I closed my eyes.

When she finished the song, we sat in silence. Father put down his blade and came to sit near us. He looked at me intently before he spoke.

"I saw Leto and Artemis today," he began, "and I've explained that your studies will be changing."

I glanced at Mother, but her face was unreadable.

"Artemis will be coming up the hill to help you. She'll teach you to ride the mare, and you can continue your healing practice on her leg."

"But the others?" I demanded. "What about all the people that we've helped? And mother's gift is so strong—"

"They will not be coming here anymore."

His voice was stern. I shifted to my knees to look at Mother's face, but couldn't read her expression. I rolled my eyes in disbelief and was about to object when Mother shook her head slightly. I struggled to control my feelings of protest.

"Understand me, Hera—I don't want you going to the village until things settle down there. There are other healers in other places that will serve the community. When you're ready, someday, perhaps you'll be one of them. But not today."

He offered me no other explanation, and I knew more than to press him when his mood was severe. I would get nowhere. I nodded at his instructions and rose to my feet. He stood up too, and when I moved toward my room, he stepped into my path so that I had to face him. I looked him evenly in the eye.

"Give me your word, Hera," he said.

I opened my mouth to object, but the fierceness in his gaze stopped me.

"You will not go to the village until I give you leave."

Again, I looked at Mother, who had risen at his words and come to stand by his side.

"Your word, Hera," she echoed.

I stared at her in disbelief, but there was something in her eyes that made my anger fall away. An anxious feeling swept through me, but I nodded to them both and bowed slightly.

"I swear it," I said.

I went quickly to my room, shutting my eyes against the tears that pressed at my lids. It took me several moments to understand that the sensation that pricked my skin was fear.

CHAPTER SEVEN

MY FATHER BEGAN TO ACT STRANGELY. He often went to the village, returning with thick sacks and material to make packs, which he filled with rice and roots. In the evenings, he sewed hide into yet more packs and closed shoes.

"What is he doing, Mother? Where is he planning to go?"

"He's not certain of those things," Mother said. "He may not go at all, but it's always good to be prepared."

I watched my parents closely. Mother, too, gathered up her roots and herbs in small satchels and placed them beside his packs and bags.

I tried to ignore the apparent tension that had moved into our family, even on the night Father measured my feet for boots. On our side of the island, the weather was always warm. Even the rain was tepid on the skin. I would never wear boots here, but I held my tongue.

I let my growing anxiety rest in my time with Artemis. She came the first afternoon to teach me to ride the mare. As exciting as it was to think of riding the horse, I was intimidated by her size. Artemis had no such fears. She reached out her hand and spoke the mare's name softly. *Luela.* Artemis approached her quietly, took hold of its mane with her left hand, and mounted her in one swift movement. I smiled, delighted. She showed me how to guide the mare with pressure on her mane and to use my knees.

Then it was my turn. I approached the horse with excitement, but she shied away. Artemis shook her head. She moved toward me with a quiet, but intent stride and both the horse and I stepped forward to meet her. Artemis slid her hands around my waist as I took Luela's mane in my hand. I caught my breath at the warm sensation her touch sent through me and struggled to keep my feelings in check. Artemis seemed not to notice. She lifted me astride in one smooth movement. The horse moved uneasily from side to side, not at all like when Artemis had been riding her. My thoughts shifted quickly from Artemis's touch to the unnerving power of the animal.

"Calm yourself, Hera," Artemis called out to me. "Be easy in your heart, and she'll be easy with you."

I did as she directed and Luela moved, slowly at first, but then in spurts of speed. A beautiful awareness of the horse's spirit moved through me. I gripped her harder with my knees, and she trotted, tossing me up and down and then eased into a canter, circling the meadow. Artemis stood in the center calling out encouragement and direction.

The movement was steady, and I sank deeper against the mare's warmth until my hips held me in her rhythm. I let go of her mane, freeing my hands, and laughed into the wind. In this natural, relaxed state I felt the warmth of the life-current move through my limbs.

Afterward, we returned to the house, and I lay my hands on Artemis's leg under Mother's soft directions. She had me focus on the warmth I felt in my body, and let it reach out to unite with the warmth I sensed in Artemis's flesh. In this way, the heat, or currents, would join and I would set my intention on healing. For our purposes, Mother instructed me to focus on the thick scar on Artemis's leg. She bade me envision it shrinking, and growing thin, until I could envision the leg perfectly healed and whole, as it had initially been.

"The body knows how to heal, Hera," she said firmly. "It just requires a healer's strong and sure direction."

As I worked, the heat continued to build within me until a thin line of sweat broke out across my forehead. Even Artemis shifted uncomfortably beneath my touch. Mother shook her head, anointed our brows with her oils and told me to relax, but I could sense she was intrigued. Perhaps she didn't feel heat the way I conjured it.

In this way, we passed many days until Mother pulled out a length of woolen thread and held it up to the scar on Artemis's thigh. She smiled broadly, her eyes wide.

"It's working," she announced, "Hera, you must be dropping deep into the awareness of Artemis' bodies vibration to be bringing forward this much current. Your ability is powerful. These are tremendous results in such a short time."

I reveled in the pride I heard in her voice.

Artemis was stretched out on my sleeping mats, and she leaned forward on one elbow to see. Mother held the string against the length of the scar one more time.

"This was the length of the scar when I closed the wound," she said.

Artemis reached for my hand and squeezed it tight. The scar was now half as long as the string and indeed less pronounced than when we'd begun.

This was what I'd needed to see if I was going to confront Father and his anxiety. Clearly, I possessed the ability to heal, and my life was calling me to it. I wished he were present so that he could see it himself, but at least I had the string.

I reached out to pick up the string from the stone table beside the bed when a ripple of heat rushed through my hand and burned the tips of my fingers. I cried out but was shocked into silence as the string was suddenly consumed in an orange flame. Mother stepped back sharply, taking hold of my arm and Artemis was on her knees before it, swatting it out. In a moment the flame had disappeared, and the string lay there, half as long, singed in black. Mother and Artemis stared at me.

"What did you do?" Mother asked me sharply.

I shook my head. Sweat poured down my cheeks from my temples. My body was dripping.

"I'm not sure," I answered. "I was excited and wanted to show Father the string."

"But how did—" then she stopped short, and her eyes widened.

She grabbed at my hands, touching the fingertips lightly. They still tingled with heat. Without another word, she pulled me quickly through the house and outside. Artemis followed. I wanted to stop and ask what was wrong, what had happened, but she moved faster, half dragging me behind her. She didn't let me go until we were at the swimming hole where she pulled me right into the water. I sucked in my breath as I plunged into the cold, but it felt good, cooling the tingling heat within my aching hands. Artemis stopped at the water's edge, and I looked at her pleadingly to intercede, but her eyes were filled with concern.

Mother put her hands on my head, splashing cool water

over my brow. I shut my eyes and let the cold prick my skin until she had calmed herself. When I looked at her, there were tears in her eyes.

"Mother, it's okay," I said, "I'm alright."

She nodded, finally letting go of my hand. I followed her as she waded out of the pool and came to sit in a patch of sunlight. We took off our tunics and Mother sent Artemis to fetch us simple wraps and pitchers of water. She bade me rest until Artemis returned.

"Watch the clouds passing above you," she directed, "imagine yourself as one of them."

"But Mother—"

"Do as I say, Hera!"

I shut my mouth, startled by her tone. I tried to do as she said, but when Artemis returned, Mother sent her scurrying about for different objects that piqued my curiosity. As Artemis ran back and forth from the house, I could see that Mother was not done with me.

Once a multitude of things had been gathered, Mother bade me get to my feet and come again to the water's edge. There, she wedged a small wooden shelf across two stones that protruded near the side of the pool. On top of it, a variety of items were set: a wooden cup and spoon, a bamboo plate, and a sharp, bronze blade. Artemis stood on the other side of the pool with a pitcher of water in her hands. I stared at Mother in disbelief.

"You want me to try it again?"

Mother nodded, pulling me again toward the pool. She directed me to do whatever I'd done before, to reach out my hands, to conjure the heat. I did as she said, but nothing happened. I tried to visualize flames reaching out from my palms, but my hands only grew warm as they did when healing. I was getting tired, and we'd missed lunch, but still, Mother pushed me.

"I can't do it!" I said irritably. "What difference does this make, anyway? You said my healing abilities are strong; isn't that enough?"

I put down my hands and moved back toward the house, but Mother took hold of my arm, turning me back to the pool.

"We have to know," she said. "Was it chance, or is this something you can really do?"

"It was only a string, Mother!"

I yanked my arm out of her grasp and stepped back. She pulled herself up tall, and for a moment, she looked foreign to me. Her eyes were very dark and piercing. She stared into mine for a moment, and I recognized the look. It was the same one I'd seen Artemis use when cajoling the mare.

"This could change everything," she said. "We have to know, Hera."

My lips were drawn tight, my hands clenched.

"What do you mean?" I cried, tired and annoyed. "Mother, why are you treating me like a child? I'm a woman now, can't you see that?"

I felt the heat rise within me naturally, as if it had always been there, smoldering. It burned in my chest and branched out my arms into two rivers.

"I'll treat you like a woman when you begin to behave like one," Mother replied evenly. "The fire, Hera, call the fire! Do it now!"

I clenched my teeth and turned back toward the pool and the little altar set down there. I reached out toward the sacrifices they'd laid out upon it and opened my hand. A surge of anger took form inside of me. The bronze blade shimmered, and the wooden objects leapt into flame. I was dimly aware of Artemis stepping back involuntarily, and Mother's gasp, but I was held in the great thrall of this rising temperature. I thought of how this would shake Father and his surreptitious planning and a surge of energy shot through me.

The flames leapt higher.

The wooden shelf that held the objects began to ripple with an orange and crimson blaze. Then, all at once, my knees grew weak and the power that I'd felt in my limbs dissipated. I felt suddenly vulnerable. I reached out for Mother's hand, and she slid an arm around me, easing me again toward the water. As soon as my feet entered the pool, a wave of relief swept over me. I sat down sending ripples across the surface, which lapped against the wooden plank now sinking into the pool. The bronze blade hissed as the water slapped its surface.

Artemis still stood in the wet sand, her pitcher full of water, but she seemed unable to use it. Instead, we all stood silently and watched the fire burn until the water consumed it.

No one spoke. Artemis pulled the cinders out and dragged the thin, blackened shelf onto the grass. Mother's hands trembled as she ran her fingers over the surface.

"You can call forth the fire," she said finally. "And it came with your emotions, not from a quiet place of control."

She rose to her feet and looked at us both unhappily. Artemis stepped closer to me, protectively. Though I was sure she didn't know any more about *how* I'd accomplished this feat than I did, I sensed that she knew *what* it meant. I longed to be alone with her so that she could tell me, but Mother pulled out her oil and moved toward me.

"How do you feel? Are you weak or hurt in any way?" she asked. I wasn't. She took my pulses and then anointed me again with the oil. Then all of a sudden, she pulled me to her and wrapped me in her arms.

"I'm sorry, Hera," she whispered. "I know you're a woman now. A beautiful young woman, but you'll always be my daughter, my sweet girl."

I kissed her cheek. "I know, Mother," I said.

"Are you strong enough to go to the fields?" she asked. "We need to tell your father."

I nodded. The three of us turned and headed down the trail toward Father's taro fields. There was a solemn mood between us.

When we reached the bottom of the trail, we turned off along a path by the stream that ran through the thick fern and forest. As we neared the opening of the green, Mother stopped abruptly. We halted behind her. She held her finger to her lips then cocked her head and shut her eyes, listening. Then I heard it, too, the sound of raised voices and the sharp whinny of horses. Mother crouched down, and we followed as she moved stealthily along the trail toward the cover of trees that fringed the taro plants. As we approached the voices grew louder, and then I could see a group of women clad in dark leather tunics and boots. They all wore their hair long, but pulled back and in braids. Most were on horseback with bows drawn, and arrows nocked, while others held carved swords in their hands. A group of ten or so stood before the horses with long spears at the ready, all pointing toward a lone figure who stood calmly amidst his crops as if they were soldiers of his own.

"Father," I hissed, starting to get to my feet, but both Artemis and Mother held me down.

"Wait," Mother whispered sharply, "Let your father face them first."

"But there are too many!"

"Trust me, Hera, your father knows what to do," she whispered back and then turned to watch through the twined branches of the tree.

Artemis had pulled out the blade she kept tied to her calf, but we did as Mother directed, and only watched. A terrible anxiety seized me as a woman on horseback shouted out to Father, but he did not answer, standing calmly and still. I strained to see her face, but it was hidden beneath the black hood of her cloak. Again, she called out to him, and I caught her meaning this time.

She was looking for the healer and her daughter.

I gasped. Mother squeezed my arm tightly and again put her finger to her lips. Father's body relaxed, and his stance changed slightly. I recognized it as the posture he took when he began his tribal dances. I knew the steps too, having practiced them since I was a child. This seemed no time to take such a pose.

The next moment the black-cloaked woman threw down her hand and a woman hefted her spear, full force, at Father's small frame. He lifted his arms and rose into the air and before I could understand what happened, he was holding the spear in his hand. He thrust it into the ground. Another woman let loose her spear, which he caught and then another and another as I watched in terror.

The women still on horseback urged their mounts forward, circling him. I clenched Mother's arm feeling the heat rise within me again, but she took hold of my shoulders and shook her head. *Wait,* her eyes said to me.

Again, the woman's voice cried out demanding Father's answer, but he stood his ground. A group of women dismounted and drew their swords. As one lunged at him with her blade, he moved smoothly out of the way, spinning about in his dance-like movement and to everyone's surprise, took the blade from her hand. She seemed stunned for a moment, but then pulled out a knife from her belt, while another woman cut hard toward Father's arm. Again, he danced behind her and took her sword. As both women looked on in dismay, he hefted the swords into the ground beside the spears that lined his back. Again, he turned to face the warriors, weaponless.

There was a flurry amongst the archers who pulled back their bows and aimed, but then the black-cloaked woman called out a command.

"Enough!"

The archers lowered their bows.

The woman moved her horse to the front of the group and pulled back her hood. I heard Mother gasp.

"Master Yen Wei," the woman said as if she knew him. She didn't get down or make any gesture of friendship.

"Athena," my father said politely, "it has been a long time."

Mother turned to me. "Stay here," she said.

"No, what's going on?"

Artemis was at my side with her blade, but Mother looked fierce. She turned to Artemis. "Keep her here, hidden, do you understand me?"

Artemis put her hand on my shoulder. "We must do as your mother says," she said firmly.

Again the heat welled within me, but this time I took a deep breath to keep it in its place.

Mother rose and returned to the path and a moment later stepped out into the field and moved to Father's side. She walked calmly and with composure as if she were greeting welcomed company. Athena slid down from her horse as

Mother approached, her eyes bearing down on her. She was very tall, and her white skin was burnt red from too much sun. I strained to hear her words.

"Sophia," she said to Mother, nodding slightly.

Then, in a most extraordinary gesture, Mother kneeled down before Athena and kissed the hem of her black robe.

I saw a smile curl on Athena's lips.

Artemis tightened her grip on my arm.

"So, you lied, Sophia," Athena said as Mother rose to her feet. "You had a girl after all."

Mother tensed.

"The High Priestess of the Emerald Temple has called for her. I've come to fetch her home."

I couldn't see the look on Father's face, but even from this distance, I sensed his resolve.

"She is home already," he said flatly. "And no one is going to take her from us."

Mother shook her head and reached for Father's arm. She leaned in close and said something in a low voice. He turned and looked at her intently. I realized she had told him what had happened with the fire.

Athena seemed to realize something new was passing between them as well. She signaled her women to collect their spears and move back into formation. She stepped back a moment as if to let my parents speak. Finally, Father lowered his eyes, bowed slightly toward Mother and turned to Athena. They stepped away from the group and spoke for a long while as Artemis, and I waited anxiously.

The armed women had retreated to the stream to water their horses. Several pulled out sacks of food and passed them around while others took up stations sharpening their blades. I watched them curiously. "Who are they?" I asked Artemis.

"Most are guards, I imagine," she answered, "but the ones in black robes…I think they must be priestesses from the Emerald Temple."

The Emerald Temple. I'd heard these words before. It was a place of power and of magic, an island unto itself far from the political pressures of the temples of Caledocean. The Emerald Temple was not run by priests as the others were, but by priestesses alone. They had their own warriors and healers, their own rites and celebrations. Priestesses from the temple were held in regard, and every few years they'd travel around the island in search of girls that showed promising signs of joining them. While most villages along the coast held hopes that one among their young women might be chosen, our community was small and remote and loathed to lose a girl of any age. Rarely had a priestess ever traveled this far, let alone a group on horseback with armed guards.

I looked back to my parents. Athena reached out her hand now, and Father shook it. My parents turned back to the trail and came toward us slowly. I reached for Father as he approached and he enveloped me tenderly in his arms. My body was shaking.

We returned to the pool by the house and Mother set up another altar in the water.

"Now, repeat your act of fire, Hera," she commanded.

Father watched as I shut my eyes and reached into the turmoil of emotions that were now churning within me. I called forward the fire and threw it at the objects that were set on top of it. I felt the heat move more freely this time. Now I was tired and more than just a little afraid, and when the flames came they were softer, and my fingertips didn't burn. Artemis stepped toward me and bathed my brow with a wet cloth, and Mother pulled open her oil to anoint me.

When they stepped away, Father had turned his back so that I couldn't see his face. He stared out over the trees at the sun that now hung low in the sky.

"You're right, Tethys," he said without looking at me. His voice was tight and low. "We will have to let her go."

CHAPTER EIGHT

MY PARENTS SENT ARTEMIS HOME and bade me rest until supper time. I postponed my questions as the fatigue in my body had overwhelmed me, and I slept restlessly for the rest of the afternoon. When I awoke, it was dark. Father helped me to the table, and we ate in silence. Afterwards, Mother brought us a pot of tea, but neither of them drank any. Father fidgeted with his cup for a few moments, which was unlike him.

"Father," I began, but he put up his hand.

"Be patient, Hera," he said. "There is much for us to tell you. You will have to listen with your heart as well as your head to understand what I'm going to say."

I nodded, but I could already feel the wariness in my breast.

"It's true what I told you about my ship being wrecked off the coast of Atlantis and your mother finding me. Everything about my people from the east, our customs, and our practices is real. But the story I told you about your mother coming from a small village in the north…this is not true. I never meant to deceive you, but I had to keep something about our story hidden, something to do with your mother."

The steam from the tea in my cup rose between us. I shifted uncomfortably.

"Your mother," father continued, "Your mother, she was, she gave up—"

"I gave up nothing!" Mother said quickly reaching out to Father. He took her hand in his but shook his head. He dropped his eyes to the table.

"You gave up everything to be with me," he said. Mother started to speak, but he put up his hand. "We must be willing to tell the whole truth. We must be willing to see hard things as well as the good."

The fire popped and crackled in the hearth. Mother let go of his hand and turned to me.

"Hera, I am the only daughter of Rhea, High Priestess of the Emerald Temple. I was her heir. My given name is Sophia, and I spent all my life before your father in training to be a priestess. That is how I know the art of healing, and of speaking with the life force. That is how I know your ability to call the fire element in such a strong and willful way is a rarified gift and a sign that you must be trained in all of the priestess' arts."

I stared at my mother, incredulous. She held my gaze and waited for me to speak, but I could find nothing to say.

"My mother," she continued, "your grandmother, Rhea, forbid me to partner with your father. She refused to let me leave the temple and live a secular life unless I promised her a female heir. We fought bitterly for over a year and when I became pregnant," her voice grew very soft and strained, "When I became pregnant she insisted that I give birth at the temple and leave the child with her to raise as a priestess."

"As her heir," Father finished.

"Leave your child? You mean me, leave me?"

Mother looked at my father then, and he let out a small sigh.

"It is often done that way, Hera. In the city, in families that have wealth and hold power, one parent or another often raises the children. Very few grow up together, as a family. But this was not our way. We could never let you go."

Mother reached out to me.

"You understand that Hera, don't you? I could never let you go!"

At this, I nodded. I was hurt that this had been kept from me, but I was also aware of how deeply they loved me. I looked at them both, and tears came to my eyes. I loved them too, of course, I did, but I also felt betrayed. I struggled with the conflicting feelings.

"So, you kept me," I said, wiping at my wet cheeks with the back of my hand. "You kept me with you, but lied to me all these years about who I am, who *we* are."

Mother reached out and put her hand over mine. "It was a mistake not to tell you, I see that now," Mother said. "Please, Hera, try to understand. The truth is that we were afraid."

It was an honest and straightforward thing to say, but I could not push down the anger and resentment of so many calm and sequestered years here when I could have been one of those women I'd seen today. Those mighty warriors on horseback had left a keen impression on me.

I pulled my hand away from Mother and leaned back. She frowned, dropping her eyes to the fire.

I turned to father. "How did you get away?"

"When your mother became pregnant, she turned her back on the temple, and all her friends there, who were like sisters to her," he said. "Athena, the priestess leading the warriors you saw yesterday, she was once a dear friend of your mothers. But when your mother turned her back on the temple, Athena did not understand. When your mother came away with me, Athena followed us and took your mother back to the temple. This happened again and again. Each time we found a simple village and set up a life together, the priestesses found us and took your mother back.

"Finally, we broke our moral code and lied. With the help of a friend, I stole your mother away just before she gave birth to you. When the priestess' came for us, I hid you away and showed them a newborn boy. We told them that this would be our only child. As a priestess, your mother knows how to control her body in this way.

"So, the High Priestess let us go. We fled here, to the eastern shore. And this is why we've lived in obscurity, and I have not allowed you to travel nor did I wish word of you, or your mother's abilities to spread."

He stopped there and waited. I could hear the grief in my father's voice and see old pain on both of their faces. I tried not to react, but I was angry. I did not like being lied to. I did not like knowing that my life could have been filled with so much more.

Finally, I shook my head and got to my feet.

"You could've told me at some point," I managed to say, my frustration barely contained.

"Yes," was all that my father said.

"I need some time," I said.

Mother looked up from the fire. "Of course," she responded. "You've had a big day, Hera, go and rest. We'll answer any other questions you have tomorrow."

I nodded, feeling my body still aching from the day's events. I went to my room sliding the door shut, hard, behind me.

I awoke to a bright ray of sunlight blazing through the un-covered window. I'd slept much longer than usual. I rose slowly from my bed checking my limbs for any discomfort left over from the day before, but my muscles were loose and supple. That was a good sign at least.

I dressed quickly in a fresh tunic and ate the bowl of fruit my parents had left on the table in the main room. Looking about the small house, I felt a new wave of irritation as I thought of the wonderful freedom that those warrior priest-esses must know. The more I thought about it, the more tightly constricted I became. I felt a wall rising between me, and the two people I loved most.

How many other people had known about this or at least speculated? I thought Apollo knew or was guessing at it. And Leto, when she'd called for Mother to heal Artemis, surely she had suspected! And all the while I'd been naïve, an imma-ture child trusting in my parent's lies. The resentment rushed to my cheeks.

When I stepped outside my parents were working in the garden. Mother stood up and stretched, lifting a hand to shade her eyes.

"How do you feel, Hera?"

"I'm fine," I answered, not meeting her gaze. "I want to go to the village and find Artemis," I stated.

Father stood up and nodded his head. "We've nothing to hide from them now," he said.

"But Hera," Mother cautioned, "if you see Athena or her women, treat them with respect. They are not to be crossed. Do you understand?"

"I understand everything," I said, turning my back on her and heading to the path.

There was a rustle behind me, and in a moment my mother was at my side, her hand falling heavy on my shoulder, stopping me.

I spun around to face her.

"What?" I snapped.

She gave me a hard look.

"I know you're angry with me, Hera, and you have every right to be, but I'm still your mother. Listen to me. Athena is a High Priestess in her own right and leads the warriors of the Emerald Temple. You must do as she bids you."

I hesitated. "I thought you said *your* mother was the High Priestess?"

"The Emerald Temple has thirteen High Priestesses, and one among them is revered as High Priestess of them all. She is their leader and the political power of the temple. She holds a seat at the great council of Caledocean. But the other High Priestesses are powerful in their own ways. Make no mistake; any fully trained priestess is a formidable force. Be mindful, Hera."

I nodded my head, shrugging off her hand. I turned and walked away.

They lied to me.

This was the thought that rose in my heart and fixed itself in the crook of my chest as I strode down the beach, moodily looking for Artemis.

Now I understood why people were treating me with such deference and respect. They must have suspected who my mother was. Everyone must know the story, for news like the High Priestess's heir disappearing, had inevitably spread across the island. Yet no one had told me about it.

Not even Artemis.

I glared at people as I passed by them. Fishermen waved, but I turned my back on them. I ran the story again and again in my mind finding fault with my parents, and my feelings of anger and resentment grew stronger in my heart.

A large group had formed near the center of the village just beyond the beach. The priestesses had set up their camp here, and the villagers were gathered about to take care of them. This was the tradition, of course, for it was an honor to have the priestesses among us. Coeus and his hunters brought in the pigs, and a large group of women sat around a fire, stripping green leaves for the pot of boiling water. Bread and jam lay uncovered on the long tables that had been set about for feasting. The fishermen's outriggers were scattered across the water, and a few young men cast nets off the crest of the sandy bay. Everyone in the village seemed to be gathered here. The area was bustling with activity and celebration.

As I approached, the two black-robed priestesses whom I'd seen the following day got up to greet me. The first woman was tall and pale skinned, with a foreign look on her face. Her hair was a remarkable color of gold, and her eyes were blue, shining with confidence. She moved like a jungle cat. Her shapely hips seemed to prance with every step. There was a deep, exotic beauty about her I couldn't fail to notice.

"I'm Aphrodite," she said, crossing her palms over her chest and bowing slightly.

I forced a smile.

The other woman was younger, slight and darker skinned, like me. I could see that she came from island people, her features soft and full, her lips the deep violet that comes just before the sky turns to night. I liked her at once. She crossed her arms over her chest as Aphrodite had done and bowed. "I'm Persephone," she said quietly.

I was about to bow back when I heard their leader raise her voice behind me.

"What are you doing, Persephone?" Athena demanded. "Hera holds no rank here. She is neither priestess nor initiate. She has not earned such a gesture of respect."

The young woman looked flustered, her cheeks turning red.

"But she's the granddaughter of—"

"She's no one!" Athena snapped, her voice loud and coarse.

I saw Artemis and Apollo move from Coeus's side by the fire pit and head in my direction. Old Helene, too, had stopped her banter with a friend and, flanked by her daughters, moved toward us.

"She's royal born!" Helene called out, as if in challenge.

There was a loud round of assent from the women that surrounded her. Athena scowled and then glared at me. Artemis stood at my side, defensively. She was as tall as Athena and could stare the priestess in the eye. Athena gave her a cold and dismissive look.

To my relief, there was a loud shout behind us that broke the tension. We all turned to look down the beach where two men struggled to hold the rope of an enormous beast of a horse. I'd never seen an animal like it. The horses in our village were small creatures, used to pull carts and heavy loads. The mare I rode was not much larger. This horse was at least twice as big, white from head to tail and sleek. It pulled sharply against the ropes about its neck and pawed the sand. Its muscles undulated and swelled as it pulled against the men.

Athena became all action. She cried out to her warriors to surround the horse and then started snapping orders. In a moment, the women were on their feet bringing more rope and spears.

"It is a prize stallion brought down from the pali to honor the priestesses!" someone shouted.

People gathered around to watch as Athena, and her women circled the horse, held up their hands and crossed their spears to form a wall to corral him.

Persephone stepped beside me as they worked.

"Athena is a strong leader," she said, her tone full of deference.

I nodded. I did not want to say what I really thought of Athena.

"It's just that she doesn't have patience for those who are not committed to the temple and its work," Persephone continued.

The other priestess, Aphrodite, moved toward us, laughing out loud.

"That's a nice way of saying it, Persephone," she said.

She pushed past her friend and moved toward me, but her eyes were on Artemis's form, taking her in. Her lips were full and pink like coral, and when she smiled at my friend, I was filled with a sense of dread. She came to stand by my side.

"Athena holds your mother's betrayal against you," Aphrodite said casually, smiling at Artemis. Artemis smiled back.

"My mother's what?" I said.

Persephone interjected, "What she means is—"

"You've no idea what I mean," Aphrodite cut her off. "Don't try to make it sound pretty, Persephone when it's not." She turned to me then. "Your mother abandoned the Emerald Temple and left the High Priestess without an heir. Athena is a loyalist. I doubt she'll ever accept you."

There were loud shouts from the beach, and the horse reared high, breaking one of the cords about its neck. It lunged at the women who formed a circle around it, cuffing in the air at the spears they held. One of the men that still held the lead stumbled and fell as the horse jerked left. The beast rose up, stabbing at the air with his hooves. Athena pulled the horse back just in time for the man to roll away. Another of the warrior women pushed the other man aside and took the other lead. She was apparently more skilled as she gave the animal more rope and it quieted some.

I was enamored of the scene. My heart raced. People in the crowd shouted out to the priestesses, "Ride him, ride him!"

Someone began to beat a drum. The horse pranced back and forth, pawing again at the sand.

Athena skillfully brought the horse closer to the growing group of people, letting them shy away from his wild stance. The circle of warriors backed away slowly, widening the space between the beast, the villagers and the long expanse of beach.

Athena smiled easily and held up her hand to quiet the crowd. When she had their attention, she called out my name loud and clear.

"Hera!" she cried, "Come stand beside me."

People looked around and then opened a space between Athena and me. Helene and her women clapped their hands. I heard her hiss a taunt in the priestess' direction.

"She's royal born," Helene said again so all could hear, "and she's got the magic of our land in her as well. She's priestess enough for us!"

I was horrified by her words, but the crowd cheered and clapped and chanted my name. I looked worriedly at

Artemis, but she stood her ground beside me. Then Athena pointed at me.

"They say he is a gift for a priestess," she cried out loudly so all could hear. "For only a priestess would be able to ride him!"

Again Helene raised her voice, "Hera's our priestess!"

The clapping and encouragement began again. The crowd was growing incensed by Athena's disregard. I could see from the look on her face that she knew it was happening and yet she continued to stare at me with disrespect. It occurred to me suddenly that she was in control of this situation and the crowd was responding just as she wanted them to. Before I could begin to understand why she would do this, the horse reared again, half dragging the woman who held his other lead and a sick feeling came over me. Before I could do anything, Athena spoke again.

"If she's a priestess," her tone was sharp and succinct, "let her prove it."

My eyes grew wide, and I stepped back involuntarily, but Artemis leaned close to my ear and said in a firm, steady voice, "You can ride this horse, Hera, don't back down."

I snapped around, panicked. "What? Don't be ridiculous, look at him—"

"Listen to me," she said steadily, "find your courage, and the horse will feel it. Just hold on to him, Hera, and I can do the rest."

My eyes widened, but I said nothing. I dropped the chatter in my mind, the anger and mistrust. I looked into Artemis' eyes and nodded. I had more faith in her than I did in myself. Trust was a familiar cadence between us.

"Hera will ride the stallion!" Artemis cried out moving toward the horse.

More people moved toward us from the beach and the tents until I felt that the entire village was looking on. My palms were wet with sweat. Artemis held up her hands to the crowd to quiet them. For a moment, I thought the sound of my heart thudding against my chest could be heard until I realized it was only the sound of the drummer on the shore.

Athena held out the lead to Artemis who moved confidently into place, whistling softly to the steed. It was a hypnotic melody, gentling and kind. She moved very slowly toward the horse, and then stopped when he backed away. She signaled me to take the lead from the other woman. I tried to calm myself, but as I moved closer to the horse, my breath quickened. He was enormous, and his eyes were fierce. Artemis stood there patiently with both of us, her soft whistling dropping into a low, droning hum. People from our village moved closer, inspired with confidence and pride. They patted my back and in hushed tones urged me on.

Artemis pressed past the wall of warriors who had begun to drop aside. As if tethered to her sound, I moved with her, toward the horse, his look bearing down on me as if he could see through my form and was looking toward the invisible force I was made of. I felt strangely exposed before him, and yet, I was pleased with his interest. For the first time, my pulse calmed, and I was able to look him in the eye. There was something familiar there, something wild, but kind.

By the time I reached Artemis's side, I'd lost the sense of Athena and the crowd. My heart had stopped battering against my breast, and I felt the now familiar warmth of the life-current move through my limbs. The horse took a step toward me. It cocked its head to one side and isolated me from the crowd with its big body. For a moment I felt him take me in, measuring my merit, the stamina of my courage.

I reached out to him in the same way, looking beyond his size, and his fury until I found his noble heart that would soon hold the worth of my life.

Artemis's sound had disappeared into the beat of the waves and my heart and the horse's deep eyes. I was vaguely aware of her taking the rope from my hand and reaching out to touch the horse's face. His head pushed against her, but she leaned closer, droning until he rested his muzzle gently in her hand.

Everyone watched in silence.

Artemis reached up and slipped the rope from around his neck. Still, he nuzzled into her, the song lulling him. With one hand on his neck, she moved toward me and placed mine on his mane. My fingers wrapped tight around the white silk. I felt her hands around my waist then and heard her voice in my ear, "His name is Pegasus," she said, and with one, fluid movement, I was upon his back.

The spell was broken.

Pegasus reared and I gripped tightly with my legs, my whole body wrapped about him. He spun around and around and then broke into a run down the long stretch of sand, pounding through the white foam of the sea.

I leaned forward with excitement. Passion filled every limb as I gripped harder with my knees and clung to his mane. My hair ripped loose from its tie and flew out like a black cape behind me. Nothing in my life could have prepared me for the joy that rushed through me. I'd found freedom. My body instinctively rolled with his brazen thunder. He tore up and down the long beach, sending sea foam fanning out beside us.

The routine of my life was being pounded away beneath his hooves, my resentment and fear falling away from us.

This was what I had yearned for all these years trapped in the certainty of my future. Now, that future was unknown and unseen, and I laughed out loud in anticipation of it. Yes, I would go to the Emerald Temple. I would seize the power and adventure that was now before me.

When Pegasus finally slowed, I could hear Artemis's soft whistle rise on the wind, and we turned and walked back toward her. He pranced before the crowd and bent his head royally when I dismounted. Persephone slipped a rope around his neck, and he bobbed his head dramatically but did not pull away. I pressed my palm to his beautiful neck, and he lowered his head. With one hand over my heart, I pressed my forehead against his. Pegasus snorted softly.

"Thank you," I said in return. I raised my head and stepped away.

The crowd around us had quieted, and people were moving off toward the fires and feasting tables.

"Well done, Hera," it was Athena's voice behind me. "It seems you *may* be worthy to ride with my priestesses after all."

I turned and was confused to see her smiling mildly as if she was pleased. She held out a beautiful cord to me that was woven with a thick golden thread. Then she turned to Persephone.

"Teach Hera how to tend her steed," she commanded.

"*My* steed," I echoed.

"As long as you are worthy of him," she said. "Now follow Persephone and do as she bids you. She will be responsible for you now. Whatever you do, or *don't do,* will reflect upon her." She leaned in close to me, very close so that I could smell the scent of jasmine on her skin. "I expect much of you, Hera, daughter of Sophia. Do not disappoint me."

She stared into my eyes for another moment then turned and walked away to join her warriors at the fire.

When she was gone Helene, and the other women came forward snatching up my hands and kissing my cheeks. I looked around for Artemis, but she was not among them. As the women moved away and Persephone slid the golden rope about Pegasus's neck, I caught sight of Artemis moving into the trees. Her hand wrapped tight inside Aphrodite's.

CHAPTER NINE

FATHER TOOK ME UP ON THE MOUNTAIN the day before Mother, and I were to leave for the Emerald Temple. It was a long, silent walk to a plateau of fern and gardenia. The flowers surrounded us infusing their strong scent into my memory.

We sat and ate, and he told me the story, as he'd done when I was a child, of the love affair of the red dragon from the east and the green dragon of Atlantis. For the first time, I understood the true meaning of his words. He was the red dragon. My mother, a priestess of the Emerald Temple, was the green. He recounted the tale of the dragon's flight and hiding of the single golden egg she laid, in her emerald temple.

When he finished the tale, we sat in silence, as was his custom, but I was restless inside. I knew he was trying to say goodbye and that the story was his way, but it was not mine. I reached out and took his hand. He looked at me, startled, but didn't pull it away. He held his arm outstretched, stiffly.

"I love you, Father," I said, my voice low and tight.

I struggled with the emotion I felt. My chest hurt. I'd been so self-centered in these last days I hadn't realized what the journey meant for my family and me. I wasn't sure when I'd see my father again.

"And I know that you love me," I continued.

He nodded and his eyes relaxed, which softened his face. "That is good," he said.

His arm was still stiffly extended, but he squeezed my hand gently. I tried to memorize the warmth of his palm against mine, and the calm, subtle strength I perceived through his touch. After a few moments, he reached for his pack and pulled out a long, thin object wrapped in leather. As he unwrapped it, I caught my breath. It was the dragon blade he'd given me on the day of the hunt.

"Apollo pulled it from the boar and brought it back to me," he said. "But the blade is for you, Hera."

I traced the deep images carved into the handle, the traces of green and red subdued, but still evident on the dragons' faces and wings. He pulled out a beautiful leather belt with a sheath attached for the blade. I strapped it about my tunic, and the blade fell below my hip, the hilt glinting in the sun.

"Eternal, immortal," Father said, his eyes resting on the dragons. "Find the dragon within you, Hera. Rest always in that awareness, and *you shall live forever.*"

A flock of grouse flew suddenly through the fern as he finished and his words seemed to echo all around me. A cold chill swept over my body, and a strange sensation pricked my skin. I shuddered.

"Hera," Father's hands were on my cheeks. "What is it, are you OK?"

I nodded and forced a smile, but a feeling of dread still lingered.

He stood up and pulled me to my feet. In a soft, quick movement Father enveloped me in his arms.

"All is well," he said. "All is well, my daughter."

We gathered our things and hiked back down the mountain towards home. When we arrived, Mother was waiting for us, but instead of coming inside, she took Father's hand and pulled him toward the field. She had a woolen blanket beneath her arm.

"It's a warm night," she noted, leading him away with a smile.

I watched them move through the meadow, his arm wrapped around her shoulder and her body pressed close beside him. The image of two swans rose to my mind, and for a moment I felt sad. Standing alone I surveyed our little home, the ripe garden beside me and the green acre round us. I breathed in the scents of plumeria, jasmine, and honeysuckle, which lay heavy in the air about me. I had been rebelling against this little paradise for my whole life, but now I perceived the truth. This was home, and I had been safe here. I had been deeply held by the two of them, and this temple they had created.

As my parents crossed the stream and slipped out of sight, my emotions flowed freely, and I wept, wondering for the first time if I would ever feel as protected, and loved again.

When Athena came for me, her warriors were on their horses stretched in neat rows behind her. Several of them led packhorses laden with tents, food, and water. Father was not there. I searched the edges of the field from atop Pegasus, but only Mother rode up beside me on the old mare. She laid a hand on my leg.

"He's always with you," she said. Still, I glanced determinedly about the green. "Keep your eyes looking forward, Hera, and stay alert," she continued. "You ride with Athena, warrior priestess, and she will not condone emotional displays."

Pegasus stamped his hoof as if approving Mother's words. The mare shied away at the action and Mother reined her in. I'd never seen her on a horse but realized now that she must have ridden with Athena before. She sat the mare with grace and ease. None of this was new to her.

Apollo and Artemis rode up alongside us, both on sturdy steeds. They were accompanying us through the rainforest and into the Valley Of The Priestess, where we would part ways. Apollo was returning to the temple of healers at Caledocean, and Artemis wanted to see the great city before she returned home. As Artemis had been at Aphrodite's side since they'd met, I was pleased to see her reining in beside me.

Athena gathered us together giving us strict instruction on pace and formation. She glanced at Mother who sat the old mare beside me.

"Sophia, do you really think your horse will be able to hold position at the front?"

Mother's old mare barely came up to the shoulders of Athena's warhorse and Pegasus was a full shoulder height taller. I glowered at Athena. She seemed not to notice.

"You could always bring up the rear," she continued.

"We will do our best, Lady," Mother said, but her voice was tight.

I felt a surge of indignation but held my tongue.

We moved out in a long formation through the village, two horses astride, and then in single file along the old Queen's road that snaked above the coast at the base of the volcano. We camped on long stretches of beach in the evenings, until the road wound upwards, leaving the familiar tropical tangle of green behind. Vast expanses of open land stretched out before us, and to my amazement, the road opened up and widened as well. We soon rode four horses astride, with Athena and her captain at the front. She led us through the countryside, skirting small villages as we went, even if it took us far out of our way. Mother explained that Athena would not want to inflame rumors that the High Priestess of the Emerald Temple had an heir before she delivered us safely to my grandmother. It was up to Rhea to decide how and when to make the announcement.

I grew annoyed as it seemed the days became a relentless routine of hiding me from the world. Even from a distance, I could see that these villages and towns were different from my own, with tall buildings of stone and strange animals that grazed nearby. It was unfair that I couldn't explore them. At night, we could sometimes hear music rising from a town just over a hill, and I longed to run towards it, to meet new people and dance. Instead, I found myself confined to a tent and often isolated from the other priestesses and warriors. What had started out as my quest for adventure had quickly become a long, and monotonous journey, under Athena's hard command. Even more annoying was that in the evenings, I had to endure Artemis's absence as she slipped away from our fire and joined Aphrodite beneath the stars.

When finally we needed supplies, Athena had us set up camp in the woods above the great town of Delian. Early the next morning she sent four women dressed in plain tunics and worn cloaks, into Delian to get us fresh supplies. They left at dawn with empty packhorses and would not return until dusk.

As I watched them go, I resolved to follow and discover the wonders of this town for myself. It was the perfect moment and a harmless plan, for the other women would be in the forest foraging and hunting. No one would miss me.

The others went about their familiar morning tasks, fortifying tents, gathering wood and taking the horses for water. As Mother took every opportunity to be away from Athena, she had made it her habit to wander afield looking for herbs. I'd often accompany her, or hunt with Artemis and Apollo. On that morning, as mother lifted her herb basket, I reached for my spear.

"I'll be with Artemis," I said, and she nodded, smiling.

When she'd left our tent, I laid down the spear, and opened Mother's pack, taking out her old wool cloak. It was a bit rough and faded, but it was warm, and I'd blend in. I slipped it into my herb basket and left the tent.

Artemis stood by one of the fires, her spear in hand. She waved to me, but I lifted my basket in response, smiling, and headed toward the trees. I did not look back lest she approach me for if anyone would guess my deceit, it was she.

The camp was hidden from the town by a dense mass of trees, but I'd seen the top of its domed buildings before we left the main road, so I knew what direction to head in. When I broke through the tree line, it was just a short distance down the hill, and there was a good, wide road to walk on. It was already filled with people, carts, and horses heading to town. Pulling Mother's cloak about me, and lifting its hood to my head, I joined them.

People talked to each other and laughed as they went. They lifted their hands in greeting as I passed. I smiled in reply, winding my way through a farmer's herd of goats, and past small outbuildings. As I got closer to Delian, I could see the tightly packed maze of stone structures in the town. I stopped and stared at the remarkable colonnaded portico of marble columns, gilded in bronze, which surrounded the central building at the heart of the town, came into clear view. People congregated about it in masses, and the wide streets outside were filled with booths and merchants. My parents had given me some metal coins in a thread-worn pouch before I'd left and they jingled at my side. In the village, I'd never needed such things, but Father had explained that they were used to trade for goods in larger towns all about Atlantis.

As I neared the gates, I fell in with a small group of women carrying baskets of bread. I gripped my basket tighter as I passed by the armed soldiers that stood on either side. They were tall, dark men with broadswords at their hips, but they paid little attention to those that passed by.

Staying close to the women I entered the town with no question or interest from them. I followed the women through the wide streets laid out in a rectangular plan. The houses we passed were very unusual to me, made of wood and mud brick, and on their roofs were hung thick terracotta tiles. Big, heavy doors of wood swung open as people came and went, crossing over marble thresholds that were framed with columns. Walls held intricate mosaics of intense blue and green. Beautiful statues of animals stood at every crossroads. I marveled at the gardens and courtyards, which I glimpsed through the open doors. All about me people laughed and chatted in a friendly manner and soon, I found myself moved with the crowd toward the center of town.

Finally reaching the tall colonnades I'd seen from the hill, I noticed that the building was set up high and a wide array of steps led to its entrance. Today, these steps were acting as some sort of stage, and a large group of men was set upon it. They wore white tunics with wide, red badges about their waists and they lined the steps with spears in hand. They were a handsome bunch, well tanned, fit and jovial. At the center, stood a young man, a head taller than the rest, his hair short-cropped and black as night. He wore a thick gold chain about his neck with a medallion that shone brightly in the sun. At his wrists and ankles, he wore bronze cuffs that made him look ready to do battle. People were crowded about him, leaning forward as he spoke about war. Young men clamored to be close to him, but his companions kept them a few steps below, their spears outstretched. I could feel the excited hum of the women around me as they admired the men on the stage.

"That young man," said one beside me. "He's got such an air about him!"

"And handsome," another added.

"My boy's going with him," an elder interjected, "he's signed up for the fight. From the way he talks, I think he'd follow Zeus anywhere!"

Zeus. The name sounded familiar.

"He's such a charmer," another went on. "The girls follow him about, you know, and any would be proud to say they'd taken a child from him."

There was a loud applause, and I turned to see the man they spoke of holding up his hands as the crowd chanted his name.

"Zeus, Zeus, Zeus…" they went on and on until he took a bow and stepped aside pointing to the tables where men sat with scrolls and quills.

"Come, make your mark and put on a uniform," Zeus called out as a long line of young men moved toward the tables.

A big man with a blond beard moved to Zeus's side and slapped him on the back. He leaned in close and whispered something in Zeus's ear, and the two men laughed. I was sure they were congratulating themselves. Still, my eyes lingered on Zeus.

There rose a rustling in the crowd around me, and I overheard one of the women say in an excited tone, "There here, close to town. Priestesses from the Emerald Temple!"

Pulling my cloak close to me, I dropped my head and hurried toward an open door. I paused just inside the door as it took several seconds for my eyes to adjust to the dim light. I had entered a long, narrow room, set full of tables and wood benches with a long wooden table across one wall and a hearth that held a pot boiling with some sort of stew. The aroma was strong and sweet, making my mouth water. People were crowded around the tables eating from wooden bowls and drinking from large pitchers of ale. They talked loudly, and there was laughter throughout the room. It was hot inside, and I let down my hood and pulled back my cloak.

Two men brushed by me and I stumbled further inside, making my way toward the woman by the hearth who was filling bowls with stew and plates with mutton.

"Excuse me," I began, but she looked at me oddly, her eyes moving up and down over my form.

"There's no work for you here, girl," she said flatly.

I shook my head. "No, I'm not looking for work," I said. "I'd like a bowl of stew and some ale, that's all."

"You got coin?"

I nodded, pulling out the bag tied to my belt. I opened it and let a few of the smaller ones spill into my hand, not sure how these pieces of metal could be equal the worth of a meal. She snatched two from my palm.

"Put that purse away," she snapped at me then. "Best not to tempt men like these."

I did as she said and looked about me. The place was filled with somewhat rough looking soldiers. A few women were moving past the tables, but I could see they were serving food and drink, and the men didn't think twice about touching them as they went. The woman thrust a bowl and a mug at me and motioned to sit near her at the table. I obeyed, feeling suddenly out of place and vulnerable.

"Men are changing," she muttered. "There was a time when they respected women, you know," she finished shaking her head. "Eat and be on your way. This is no place for a maiden."

The stew was warm and sweet with herbs I'd never tasted. The ale was strong, but I liked the warmth it spread as I gulped it down. When I stood to leave, my head filled with a sense of motion and I stumbled. Strong hands grabbed my arms and righted me. Two men leered in my direction.

"Go on now," the woman at the hearth ordered me in a loud, firm voice. "On your way, girl!"

I moved as quickly as I could across the floor and back out into the light and the busy square. My head buzzed. I pushed through the merchants, fingering their wares, laughing at the sights and sounds until my head began to throb. The drink had been much stronger than anything I'd had before. The day had grown hotter. The sweat slid down my neck and between my breasts. I took off Mother's robe, feeling faint. There was a fountain at the center of the square, and I sat down beside it, splashing fresh water on my face and cupping some to my mouth. Still, my head was alive with a dull ache and hum. I sat for a while, watching people in the market, delighted by the beautiful clothes and wares that passed by.

When I felt better, I explored the stalls myself, but the ale still made me off balance and light headed. I knew I'd done too much.

I made my way, as best I could, through the streets away from the square and back the way I'd come, but before I reached the entrance, I felt the swooning sensation again. Turning sharply down a narrow street I headed toward the familiar scent of the stables. The smell of horses relaxed me, and I moved between the stalls to the back of the open aired barn. I was relieved the town's people were so engaged in the festivities of the day and hoped they would leave the stables alone.

Behind the last stalls, I put down my cloak on a small pile of hay and lay down gratefully. I dozed lightly, hearing the soft breath of the horses all about me. A few people came and went in the stalls near the street, but no one came upon me. I slept deeply, then, my body resting, my mind oblivious except to the darkness in which I floated.

Then I dreamt.

It was a gentle dream at first, just an image really, but one so strong and vibrant that I seemed to wake up inside of it. There was ship on a wild sea, and men threw about the deck as the sea rocked them to and fro violently. But on the bow of the boat stood a man, tall and regal, his dark hair bound behind him. I seemed to move with the wind, which circled the ship, pushing it up against the waves and then down the other side. The men cursed, and some were thrown over the side. And yet the man stood still, alone, his body facing the storm as if he was a fixture that couldn't be moved by it. He was fearless, his azure cape sweeping behind him in the wind like a set of wings.

I moved above him, and then beside him, in the impossible way dreams allow, and he followed me with his eyes as if he could see me. I wanted to see his face more closely, I reached out, struggling to make out his features, but the wind claimed me too, and I was torn about the scene. All I could glimpse in detail were his eyes.

Sapphire blue.

The intensity of his stare moved through me so that I called out, waking with a start.

I sat up in my makeshift bed. My head seemed my own again. A breeze moved in through the open front of the barn, and I loosened my tunic down over my shoulder so the breeze could cool me. I drank from my flask of water and settled back into the hay trying to remember the man's eyes, his look, to ferret out the meaning of such an intense dream.

There was a rustling in the stables, and I drew myself up. Two men approached one of the stalls near me. They were speaking excitedly and didn't notice my presence.

"Here they are," one said, his voice rough. I glanced at the pile of hay, making out his features. He was the big man with Zeus that I'd seen earlier that day. Beside him, Zeus was climbing over the stable wall. The horses moved sideways as he landed in their stall, but he put out a gentle hand and soothed them.

"You're wrong, Orion," he said patting down one of the mares. "These horses aren't fine enough to belong to the Emerald Temple. Besides, what would priestesses be doing all the way out here?"

I caught my breath.

"I tell you, Zeus, they've found the girl, and they're bringing her back to the Emerald Temple."

"A true heir," Zeus said. "This will put Hades' plans on hold! My brother's going to be in for a rude surprise after all his wooing of Demeter's daughter when now there's one above her!" Zeus laughed, bounded back over the stable door and landed easily on his feet. "I've still got a chance to rise above him," he said patting his friend on the shoulder, grinning.

His teeth were straight and clean, and his chin dimpled as he smiled. I liked the playfulness in his eyes. I strained forward trying to make out their color. The hay bed upon which I leaned was too soft, and in a moment, I toppled out from my hiding place. I stumbled to my feet, staring wide-eyed at the two men who moved quickly to my side.

"What are you doing there?" Orion growled, grasping hold of my arm firmly.

His grip was too strong, and it hurt me.

"Let go of me!" I demanded. I straightened up and pushed hard against him, but he only squeezed tighter.

I looked up at him, intimidated by his size, but I repeated it in an imperious tone. Zeus put his hand out to Orion and bade him let me go.

"What harm can she do us?" he said in a jovial tone.

The larger man seemed to think on it for a moment before he loosened his grip and let me go. I fell backward a step, or two then righted myself. Orion leered down at me as I pulled my tunic up over my shoulder.

"She's a pretty one, isn't she?" he said to Zeus as if looking at a horse.

His intention was clear before the words moved beyond his lips. My hand moved to the hilt of the knife on my belt, and in one long, swift movement, I pulled it sharply from the sheath. The blade sliced upwards across Orion's tunic. His eyes narrowed, and he lifted his hand, but Zeus shouted a stern command and thrust his body between us.

Orion stepped back hissing at me. "Stupid girl."

In a moment, Zeus snapped an order, and Orion stormed back through the stable and out onto the street. Then, Zeus turned to me.

"Are you alright?" he asked gently.

I nodded, keeping my blade exposed between us. He smiled kindly. "I'm sorry," he said, nodding in Orion's direction. "My soldiers are not always well behaved."

Still, I kept the blade in my hand.

"What's your name?" he asked.

I hesitated. "Juno," I said. It was a tribal version of my name by which my father used to tease me. Just evoking it made me think of him and this gave me courage. Slowly, I sheathed my weapon. He smiled at that.

"Why were you spying on us, Juno?"

"What? I wasn't, I mean—" I tried to deny it, but the truth was evident.

Now that we were standing together, alone, I took a moment to take him in. He was quite tall and square-faced, and his eyes were a pale color of blue. The image of my dream flashed before me. The desire to reach out and touch Zeus, as I had wanted to feel the man in the dream, moved over me.

"I wanted to see the color of your eyes," I said honestly.

He seemed surprised by my words and then delighted. He laughed.

"Well, now you've seen them," he said. "What do you think?"

I stared up into the two pale blue pools and smiled. I was strongly attracted.

"I think I wish I had more time to get to know you," I said boldly.

Maybe it was still the ale, or the spark I'd felt in the dream, or the warm, raw heat of the day, but a powerful desire to be free and enfolded in pleasure overcame me. Why shouldn't I indulge myself? I'd done everything they'd ordered me to do, why not take advantage of this little moment and satisfy my own desire. The thought that I was free to do so, and in this strange place with this handsome stranger sent a thrill through my body. I smiled at him with warmth and favor.

Zeus had obviously seen that look before. He glanced down at my makeshift bed on the straw and then back to me.

"There's still plenty of time in the day to get to know me better," he said. "People won't return to the stable until late in the day."

He reached out a big hand and stroked my cheek. A pleasant sensation moved across my skin. I caught my breath and stepped toward him. His eyes held me for a moment with a quizzical expression. For a moment he felt familiar, as though I'd known him for a very long time. As he stared at me, I sensed he was feeling something similar and was struggling to name it.

"You're very beautiful," he said almost to himself, "you have the look of the tribes about you. It's here, in your eyes."

Again, he reached out and touched my face.

"My father," I said.

He seemed to like that. He took a step closer. I could smell the barleywine, sweet on his breath.

"My mother, too," he offered, "she's from Minoa, an island in the Aegean."

I leaned forward as he spoke, lifting my head and parting my lips, inviting him to kiss me. He bent his head and pressed his lips softly to my mouth. A flood of images pressed themselves upon me. Images of the sea, a storm, blue eyes and dark hair accosted me. I pulled away catching my breath, but my body was flushed. I was overcome by the strong sensation I felt for this young man whom I didn't even know! The strangeness of it thrilled me. There was an abandon in it, a voyage I'd never taken before. He placed his palms on my cheeks and kissed me again, this time long and slow. Then his hands were on my waist, and his lips found my neck. He said the name I'd given him, "Juno," he whispered, and the anonymity of it freed me.

After a few minutes, he stopped and pulled away. I looked up at him with surprise, but he shook his head.

"There is something about you," he said. "I feel like I already know you." His voice was soft and genuine. The charming guise had dropped away, but this only made him more attractive.

"I am being too forward. There's no need to rush or give ourselves to each other here, in the stables. I possess fine apartments I will bring you to…"

"No," I said abruptly.

He stepped away, taken aback. I laughed, realizing he wasn't used to hearing that word. I glanced outside. The sun was still high in the sky, there was plenty of time, and it had been such a long time since I'd been with a lover. Just because Artemis would not take me, did not mean I had not explored with others, and I knew the intense pleasure a good man could bring me. My body moved toward him, and my hands slipped up around his thick neck, drawing him back in.

"I mean you're not too forward," I corrected, pressing my body close to his. "I want you now, right now," I finished, letting the smooth curve of my lips brush against his.

I awoke a few hours later, lying languidly in the crook of his arm. My skin was warm against his and the scent of our sex, like salt and sea, hung close about us. He was breathing deep and slow, still asleep, but his hand rested protectively across my breast. I smiled, nuzzling my lips gently against his neck and kissed him. He didn't rouse. Shifting onto my elbow, I looked down at him. His strong features were soft in sleep. There were thin lines around his eyes that I thought must be as much from laughing as from his command. His brows were thick and dark like his hair, his nose high-bridged and prominent. I thought his skin was very white, uncommonly so, but his cheeks held the bright red look of work beneath the sun. I let my eyes trace his body, so new to me and yet...I felt a deep sense of comfort.

The sound of laughter echoed down the long row of stalls, and I reached for my tunic. Zeus stirred. The laughter died down, but I could distinctly hear voices. People were taking their horses from the stalls. I glanced beyond our nest of hay out to the sky and had a sinking feeling. The sun was nowhere to be seen. I reached for my tunic and pulled it over my head, quickly, then reached for my belt, but Zeus was awake, his hands firmly on my hips, pulling me back down.

"Where do you think you're going?" he said, amusement in his voice.

He kissed me long and slow. My mouth opened to him. I felt the warmth in my legs as he pushed them apart.

"I can't," I mumbled, "It's late."

His lips were on my neck, warm, lingering. The sound of his voice was soothing.

"I'll help you explain it," he said. "I'll take you home."

I tensed, but he didn't seem to notice. Pulling his face to mine, I kissed him again and then roughly pushed him away. I rolled out from under his bent arm and strapped on my belt.

"Help me look for my leggings," I directed in a hurried glancing up at the darkening sky. "I really am late," I said. "I had a wonderful time, but my mother's waiting for me."

He was relaxed still, slowly pulling his tunic over his head. Hay tumbled from his hair. I brushed my tresses to free them from the long, thick pieces of straw. A vague sense of anxiety was rising as I realized I might not make it back to camp in time.

"Don't worry. I'll come with you. You'd be surprised at how mothers love me."

He combed through my hair with his fingers, pulling out the golden threads of hay. I laughed at him and shook my head, reaching for Mother's cloak. He looked at me quizzically.

"You're so arrogant, Zeus," I said plainly, kissing his mouth as it puckered in a pout of protest.

"But it's true," he insisted, pulling me back and facing me in earnest. "Your mother will know who I am, surely, and that will quiet her fears."

I nodded obligingly, but couldn't repress another smile.

"I'm a Titan, you know," he said then, suddenly earnest. I sat down and pulled on my boots. "Really, Juno, people know who I am!"

I stopped for a moment, surprised as much by his tone as by the use of my new name. I wished I'd told him my own, but now it was too late and of little use. I'd never see him again, anyway. He crouched down beside me, his hand gently brushing my cheek, but I pulled away and got to my feet. The sky had surrendered its pallor of daylight blue, and the purple twilight was now upon us. Mother would know I was missing by now and would surely be worried.

Zeus got to his feet, pulling his own cloak about him and made to leave with me, but I put up my hand and placed it firmly on his chest.

"Thank you," I said gently, but with intention. "But I will leave alone."

I kissed him again, and despite myself, I let my lips linger. He pulled me to him, and his voice came low in my ear.

"When can I see you again?"

I shook my head. This was becoming difficult. It was clear he wasn't the sort of man who would settle with one woman, and I hadn't really thought he'd expect to see me again.

"I have to go," I said pulling away. "Really, Zeus, it was so nice—"

"Nice?" His brow furrowed. "Being with me was *nice?* Juno, I feel more than that. You seem… different somehow. I want to see you again."

I sighed. He kissed me again, and his hands were persuasive, but the sounds of horses being led from their stalls and the chatter of people returning from their day kept me alert and steadfast. I tried to pull away, but he held me close as if he were in need.

"If it's meant to be, Zeus, I'll see you again."

He protested, but I shook my head. "Let me go now," my voice was firm and low.

He released me. "I'll look for you tomorrow," he said.

I reached out and took his hand in my own and kissed it. Our eyes locked. Again, I felt a strange pull toward him, and the image of the man in the dream pressed on my vision. Then I let him go, and turned and ran through the stables toward the town gate. I didn't look back. The sky was growing dark above me, and the streets were filled with people, carts, and horses. I pushed my way through until I reached the open road and the fields that led toward the tree-lined hill. I hurried past the farmer's plots and the empty field where sheep had been grazing that morning. Now, it was growing cold and late, and the herdsman had gathered them all in. I stumbled as the light continued to fade, but made my way steadily up the winding road. When I reached the top, I considered taking to the trees, but the light was fading so fast, and I feared I would be lost in the forest. The road would take longer, but it was the safer route. I turned and took one last look at the town, glistening with a warm orange glow from the evening lights. Then my eyes fell upon a band of torches moving through the gate. There were shouts from the men just outside of it, as the riders sped by at a frightening pace. There were eight or so, with torches blazing above their heads. They moved toward the road in a steady formation. Even as they took the first wide turn, the horses stayed abreast of each other in a perfect arrangement.

I froze. These were not average riders. I could hear them thundering up the hill, drawing closer, and I looked again to the tree line, thinking I might still be able to return to camp unseen, but it was now far too dark. My body shivered with the cold. The horses took another turn below me. Whoever they were, they'd be passing me in moments. I moved into the grass just off the road, my boots growing wet from the evening dew. I put my hood up and gathered the warm folds of Mother's cloak about me, keeping my gaze down, but even before they topped the hill, I knew they would recognize me, for I was the one they sought.

CHAPTER TEN

THE HORSES CAME UP FAST BEHIND ME. The light from the orange blaze in the women's hands cast their shadows like fiends across my path. I stopped, turned and looked up into the eyes of the woman on the big gray that pulled up sharp beside me.

Athena's voice was terse, "Hera, are you alright?"

She slid from her horse's back and was by my side in two quick bounds, her captain at her side holding the torch up high. I nodded but stood quietly.

"Where've you been?" she demanded.

I didn't answer straight away. I wasn't sure how much to say. To any other woman in her troop, I might have told a quick half-truth, but Athena was different. She would ride me hard and to steer away from her anger seemed reasonable.

"I lost track of the day," I began, but my voice faltered. "I wanted to see the town."

Her brows snapped up as I spoke. "You wanted to see the town? The *town?*"

The woman beside her moved uneasily, and I caught the slight shake of her head. Athena clenched her jaw and narrowed her eyes. Then she signaled her captain with a nod of her head, and the captain called for a horse, gesturing for me to mount. I did as she instructed. Another woman nudged her mount forward and took my reins. Athena was quickly astride her gray, snapping orders to the rest.

"Call off the search," she said briskly. "And bring the women out of the trees."

My shoulders sagged. So, they'd been out looking for me, of course. I'd been such a fool to stay gone so long and to indulge in my own pleasure.

"You're unruly," Athena muttered as she wheeled her horse around and faced me. "Half the Atlantean foot army's camped just on the other side of the town, Hera, and the Titan dynasty is leading them. They're no fools. They know we're here now and soon enough will know what we're about."

"But why are we hiding?" I countered.

She regarded me then. She sat atop her fidgeting horse lightly, as though it didn't exist beneath her. It was the first time I recognized true power in her eyes and understood what Persephone had told me of her brilliance as a commander. Athena looked straight through me, judging me to a hairsbreadth, assessing my strength, weakness, and honesty. I moved uneasily under her gaze.

"The leaders of the dynasties seek power over the Emerald Temple, Hera. I thought you understood that?" She paused, but I waited for her to continue before replying. "You knew we were avoiding such communities, you knew—" she stopped, catching the anger rising in her own voice.

I sensed the danger here. She had a passion, but it wasn't unleashed. There was wisdom here, too, and a higher purpose to which she was bound. Still, the mention of the Titans unnerved me. How could I now confess to having not only disregarded her orders and stolen away but to have also taken the Titan, Zeus, as a lover?

Athena moved her horse forward, signaling the woman at her side to raise the torch. She stared at me intently, and I knew she sensed my unease.

She spoke quite pleasantly then, without the heat. "Where have you been?"

"Just in the town, walking about, seeing things—"

"Who did you meet?"

I shook my head slowly and tried to hold her gaze. As I sat on the big mare, we were eye to eye.

"What do you mean?"

She spurred her horse suddenly, right up to my mare. She leaned forward, taking hold of the folds of my cloak at the neck. I tensed at the movement, but she gripped tighter, half-lifting me from the saddle. She thrust her face close to mine as the horses stamped and sidled together. She spoke through clenched teeth, her voice breaking with temper. "The fate of the feminine face of the divine may lie in your hands, Hera, and you don't even have the fortitude to speak the truth and stand by your deeds." She almost spat the words.

She let go of my cloak so that I fell back into the saddle, gripping my horse's mane. The torch was still high above me. Athena reached toward my shoulder and pulled forth a long, thick piece of straw that was still half tangled in my hair. Then she turned her back on me, and spurred away, our horses falling in line, instinctually, behind her, into the night.

When we arrived back at camp, no one mentioned my escapade or my disheveled state. I was taken to Mother's tent, where two guards were now posted in front and behind.

When we were alone, Mother handed me some bread and a mug of water and took out her turtle shell comb. I ate in silence, waiting for her to ask where I had been, but she said nothing as she pulled at my long, dark strands and smoothed out the curls. The sounds of horses' hooves tromped by in the distance as women continued to return from the search. I felt miserable.

"I wanted a little adventure," I offered.

Mother continued to pull at my hair, beginning a single braid down my back. My stomach churned, and I couldn't touch the bread.

"I didn't mean to upset anyone!"

"You were thinking of only yourself, Hera. You have no excuse, so make none," Mother said flatly.

Tears rose up in my eyes. The look on Athena's face lingered in my mind, and her biting words, *the fate of the feminine face of the divine may lie in your hand...* what had she meant by that? The rest of her words weren't lost on me. I knew I couldn't mention Zeus, and that I'd have to find out more about the Titan dynasty. I had so many questions, but every time I asked Mother she deferred to the future, telling me to wait until we reached the Emerald Temple. Everything would be revealed then.

"If anyone would have explained things to me," I said defensively, but Mother stopped me short.

She put down the comb and laid a heavy hand on my shoulder.

"I thought it was enough to tell you to wait," she said. "I thought you'd trust my word and obey me."

I dropped my head in disgrace. She was right of course. I'd been brought up to respect my parents' words and wisdom. I knew I wasn't the only one I'd brought shame upon this day, and I regretted that my mother and kind Persephone would have to face Athena as well.

"I'm sorry," I said.

Mother said nothing. She handed me the comb and strode out of the tent.

We left just before dawn, packing by torchlight, to escape the area before the townsfolk or the army could stop us. Athena made it plain that our presence was known; so she took to the main road for it was the most direct way to the temple. There was no point in hiding now. She led us as fast as she dared ride, past the town and the low field where the Titan foot army camped. The sun was rising as we passed, making the camp visible. Long rows of tents, evenly spaced, gave the impression of several hundred warriors. The rows of tents were marked by the movement of early morning campfires being lit. Men leaned on spears and watched us as we passed. I pulled the hood of my cloak up around my face as we went by, hoping Zeus and his friend, Orion, were safely sequestered in the town. Artemis rode beside me and noted my movement. She glanced at me quizzically, but I didn't meet her eyes. It was difficult to face any of them after they'd lost an entire day looking for me. I could feel my shame as if it was painted on my skin.

We passed by without engagement, but I didn't let down my hood until they were half a day behind us. Every time we stopped to rest or gather supplies, women were assigned to follow me about. After several days of strict obedience and tolerance of the women's presence, I protested, but Mother silenced me. They were there as much for my protection, she assured me, as to assist me in staying on course.

Needless to say, my adventure out into the world, and into what I had thought would be freedom, wasn't what I'd thought it to be. A heavy sense of the importance of the journey settled in my mind. I became careful to obey Athena's every word, to assist Persephone and Aphrodite in their chores and rituals and to stay close to Mother when we weren't riding. Still, the guards were with me constantly.

After a full fortnight of travel at a strong and steady pace, we'd passed from our jungle home through the high grasslands of the volcano and journeyed down along the river into a broad valley. The terrain was entirely different than the hills, and although the evenings were cool, there was no need of tents to shelter us from rain or animals when we slept. Everyone's spirits lifted as we entered the valley, and I knew we were getting closer to the Emerald Temple. To the north lay Caledocean, a drier climate and the sea. Further inland was the Valley of the Priestess, the great lake and the island in the mist.

On the night we set up camp at these crossroads Apollo, and Artemis came to our fire to say goodbye. In the morning, I would ride with the priestesses toward the temple, and they would take the other road, to the city.

After we'd eaten and settled our sleeping mats by the fire, we stared at the flames in silence for a time. Apollo poked at the logs with a long, forked stick. Artemis sat beside me but said nothing.

"Well," Apollo began finally, as the flames died down. "We have a long day tomorrow."

He leaned over, hugging me tightly. "Our paths will cross again, Hera," he said. His tone was earnest. "I know it will be so."

I smiled and nodded dutifully, but I'd begun to question all the things I thought I knew. I had embraced this journey to the Emerald Temple oblivious of what it would cost me and of what freedom really was. I saw that now. As my friends prepared to leave me, I realized how foolish I'd been.

I hugged Apollo back and watched him walk away. The night was full of the sounds of women moving to their sleeping rolls and the shifting of wood as fires died down. Still, Artemis said nothing. The skin of her arm brushed against mine as she leaned forward to take up Apollo's stick and push the coals about.

"Shouldn't you go now, too?" The words surprised us both, coming out like an arrow of accusation.

Artemis sat back, the stick like a spear on the ground between us.

"There's still time," she said slowly.

I turned my head away, tears tight in my throat. I wouldn't let her see me cry.

"Aphrodite will be waiting for you," I said.

Silence.

"You might as well go now," I continued, "we have to say goodbye sometime."

She threw the stick in the fire and in a moment the coals made it flame. The light flashed on my face, and she put her hands on my cheeks, turning me toward her.

"It's hard to say goodbye, Hera. Aphrodite is just a pleasant distraction, a way to make room between you and me before you—" she faltered.

My jaw was clenched against the rough, but familiar skin of her palm. She let me go.

"I don't know when I'll see you again," she ventured. Her voice was soft, and I realized her cheeks were wet with tears.

I cried softly and moved into her open arms. My body shook with the fear of leaving her, of facing the unknown alone. We sat together for a long time. The fire died out. She reached for my blanket and pulled it around us both. We lay down together beneath the stars as we'd done so many times in the past, tracking animals in the green. She pointed to the stars and their constellations in the sky and drilled me as she'd always done on their placement and meaning. She scolded me when I got them wrong, and I calmed in the familiarity of our routine until I finally fell asleep beside her.

When day came and we'd broken camp, Artemis and I said good-bye. She mounted her steed and rode off with Apollo in the direction of Caledocean, and did not look back. Athena was engaged in reforming her lines. Persephone and Aphrodite had taken their place just behind her. They turned toward me with pressing looks as I stood apart watching Artemis disappear down the road, but I ignored them until my friend disappeared from my sight. Then I turned back to my duty. I mounted Pegasus and moved him forward to take my place beside them, but my mother's mare pushed itself in front of me. Mother put her hand on my reign.

"Stay close to me, Hera," she directed as we moved together toward Athena and her captain who'd taken their places at the front of the line. Athena stared at Mother coldly as she approached, her eyes falling to Mother's hand on my bridle.

"My daughter and I will leave you here," Mother said. "I give you my word, we will travel to the Temple, but we shall do so alone, and by another road."

Athena inhaled sharply and shook her head. "We're not leaving you unaccompanied," she retorted. "We are still two days from the lake, and Titan soldiers are still patrolling. I have my orders to deliver you to the temple—"

"I know the way," Mother cut her off. "We thank you for your escort, but we'll be fine on our own."

"Sophia," Athena hissed pushing her horse forward. "This is temple business! You have no rights here!"

"She's my daughter, Athena, and I am the only one here that has any right! Hera and I also have temple business to attend to. We shall go the rest of the way on our own."

I glanced at Persephone, but she shook her head slightly, signaling me to be still. Nobody moved. Even the horses were at attention.

Athena leaned forward in her saddle. "You are not leaving this party, Sophia, *not without me.*"

Mother snapped her horse around, letting go of my lead. She rose up in her saddle, bearing down on Athena's form so that their horse sidled each other aggressively, Mother's little mare pushing hard against Athena's mount.

"There was a time—" Mother began, but Athena's voice cut harshly above it.

"That time is gone!"

A surge of fear ran through me, and I pushed Pegasus forward suddenly, his large white body moving between them. Both of their horses turned and trotted back, but they were quick to right them.

"Hera," Mother called.

Pegasus moved toward her without my bidding.

Mother struggled to calm her breath and temper. She faced Athena squarely.

"I know I have given you cause not to trust me, Athena," she said. "But it was for a good reason, and you played your part in it too."

Athena clenched her jaw, grimacing.

"You're going to have to trust me now, Athena," Mother continued. "I'm taking Hera, as my own mother once took me... the *old* way."

With that, she turned her horse around and kicked her into a trot. Again, without my signal, Pegasus followed close beside her. I looked back over my shoulder expecting Athena to follow, but she only sat back in her saddle with a stern look. Her gray horse pawed the ground unevenly, and then I heard the sharp sound of her voice as she gave the order to move on. Persephone raised a hand to me slightly and inclined her head. I did the same and then turned to the road before me.

Mother had us backtrack past the river's edge and then away from it. She turned us off the road onto a dimly marked trail that I was surprised she could have seen, and we rode on through open fields until the sun was high above us. There were ancient oak trees here in groves, with thick trunks and high, shading branches. We rode between them at a fast pace.

When we slowed to rest and water the horses, I looked at Mother. Her face was still set in a harsh stare, her eyes before her, and I sensed her mood was gray. I followed in silence, keeping close to her as she had said.

We rode hard the rest of that day and just before twilight we came upon a small field in the middle of which stood a gnarled tree that looked to be made of two different types. The branches on one side reached up toward the sky, lofty, and long-limbed, while the branches on the other side drooped low and were covered with a light green moss that hung dry and vine-like to the ground. It was a strange sight, but Mother seemed to have expected it. She rode to its base and dismounted. I followed. She walked to the tree and placed her palms on the trunk, then stood there quietly. A rush of birds' wings rose from the tree's branches. Then Mother dropped her hands and stepped away.

"We're here," she said averting my gaze.

Before I could respond, she reached out for the horses' packs and pulled them to the ground roughly. Then she took hold of their leads, drawing them to the brush at the edge of the clearing from which the sound of water arose.

I set up our camp. Mother came back shortly with the horses well watered, and let them go free to graze in the field.

"You know this place," I said, as she came to the shallow, stone pit I'd carved out for the fire. I'd collected dry brush and pulled out my flint, but she stayed my hand.

"I'll do that later," she said, avoiding my question.

She moved about our small camp in an agitated fashion, pulling out food for the evening meal, but leaving it beside the bag, then bending down absently to tend our sleeping rolls.

"Mother—"

"Yes."

"Why are *we* here?"

She didn't look at me but answered, "I had a dream."

I took a deep breath, waiting for her to elaborate, but she only continued to straighten the blankets side by side.

"Where are we?" I asked.

"An ancient place," she answered. "A place of power. Around that hill, up on the other side of the crag sits the first castle of the Atlantean dynasties. The Titans used to rule from there. This used to be their sacred grove."

I let out a long breath and shook my head. "But why are we here?"

She stood up and faced me. Her eyes looked far away.

"My own mother brought me here once," she offered, but her voice trailed off. She shook her head and forced a smile. "This is a good place, Hera, a powerful place and it is a blessing to be here. There is nothing to fear in this place," she said, and then repeated it, firmly. "There is nothing to fear."

She handed me a basket. "Here, take this to the stream. You will find mushrooms and herbs growing all alongside it. Follow it down around the bend if need be. There is still a good bit of light."

I stared at her intending to protest, but the look on her face told me it would do no good. Annoyed, I took the basket. "Fine," I muttered as I trudged off into the brush and down the little hill to the stream.

When I was well out of hearing, I complained loudly that I was no more than a prisoner on this trip and now she'd ruined my chances to ride into the temple with the prominence of the priestesses. As I wound my way down the streambed, picking herbs here and there, I became more infuriated at her self-indulgent and straightforward expedition, dream or no dream, and thus failed to notice the change of light beneath the dense canopy of trees. It wasn't until the basket was half full and I'd walked a long way that I realized I was squinting and could see only by the dim light that broke through the branches here and there. The terrain was thick with foliage. Then, I heard a rustling sound. It wasn't loud, but I heard it distinctly. I spun around. Nothing was there. The rustling came again, in front of me now, but when I turned again, I saw only the thin forest ahead. A strange cry rose up out of it like an old woman wailing. As abruptly as it began, the noise disappeared. I stood still in the odd quiet, the brook slapping over the rocks a few feet away. My skin grew cold. With my free hand, I reached for the blade on my belt, holding my hand fast on the hilt. Moving forward slowly, I stepped around the curve in the brook, confident now that I wasn't alone.

A flock of birds broke the brush just before me, and I gasped. When they'd passed, I sighed and relaxed my arms. I looked down at my basket, but it was still only half full. I let my eyes fall to the ground again, but something still hung in the air that made me feel uneasy.

I moved around the small bend in the stream and stopped abruptly as the water seemed to disappear beneath large boulders that blocked the way. I looked about irritably and turned to go back, but a chill breeze rushed through the trees scattering the herbs I'd gathered. Dropping down to my knees I grasped at them as they moved lightly around the boulders. On the other side, I pulled up suddenly as I beheld the large opening of a cave that seemed hidden there. The herbs sprinkled themselves before it as if they were offerings on an altar. The stream sprung up again here, bubbling into a pool at the entrance. It wound about a giant, smooth-floored cavern then disappeared into the blackness beyond.

My eyes cast about for bones or animal tracks, but the ground was clear, and the dirt smooth. My herbs were the only things spread upon the floor of the cave.

I knew I should turn around and return to Mother, but something made me stand there, looking into the black. The birds fluttered somewhere behind me, but their sound only came into a dim part of my awareness.

I stepped inside the cave. Slowly. Quietly. The stream gurgled beside me as if it were my friend. Looking about I saw torches fitted into the side of the rock walls. Large stone jars and candles coated with dust and dirt stood beneath them. Instinctively, I reached for a torch and pulled out my flint. The handle was heavy and wrapped finely with wool and tar. The metal work on the side glistened as the flint struck the stone and flame leapt from the pitch. This was very fine craftwork, and it was equaled on the handles of each torch. I raised the light above my head, my curiosity piqued. There were old, gilded storage chests, hinged and heavy. I opened one to find fine uniforms, still folded, but when I lifted them up the cloth crumbled like dry leaves. I stepped back, disappointed. My fear of the place receded, and the thought of long-forgotten treasure enticed me. Outside the cave I could still see an orange streak of light, so I continued my exploration, opening other chests, carefully at first should vermin have made refuge here, but nothing was living inside these tightly shut trunks. One after another I pulled them opened excitedly, finding old blades, and jeweled cups. At some point, I thought I should go to Mother and bring her here to marvel at my find, but the more I opened, the more entranced with the treasures I became. Before I realized what I was doing, I had moved from chest to chest, beyond the entrance of the cave and wound deep into its belly. The stream trickled steadily beside me so that I hardly noticed when the light of the torch was all that I could see by. When I reached the last trunk and lustily threw back the lid, I was surprised to find it empty. I held up the torch, which now flickered dimly. There was a set of stairs carved into the jagged stone before me that rose up and up, past the glow of my light. I realized I must be beneath the old palace, or in some hidden entrance to its temple.

Turning around, I looked back the way I'd come, the long tunnel disappearing into the darkness. I shivered. What had I been thinking? I dropped my basket again, the gilded cups, beads and tortoise shells that I'd collected spilling about my feet. The torch flickered and sputtered, and I realized it was about to burn out. I looked frantically at me for another torch to light, but there was none. My palms sweated. The darkness seemed to close in all around me. My breath changed in the echoing cavern to short, quick gasps as the flame sputtered and then went out.

Panic overwhelmed me and my limbs shook.

"Steady yourself, Hera," I said out loud. The sound of my voice reverberated all about me.

I pressed my hand up against the wall and shut my eyes to help calm my senses. When I opened my eyes again, the blackness was complete, and I lost myself in it. The directions faded into one. There was nothing here but the cold, damp chill of the place, the frantic sound of my breath, and the agitated bubbling of the stream.

I wanted to scream.

Suddenly, something moved in front of me. Something in the thin, frightening space around me, changed. My skin pricked, and I gasped as a pale light began to shimmer. A form took shape, a woman, old but familiar, reaching out to me kindly.

"Don't let your fear overcome you, Hera," she said.

I couldn't tell if my eyes were open, or closed, but her body was glowing, a light in the darkness. Her face became clearer, and her glinting eyes sparked a memory. I recalled the dream from that night of formless travel, and the old woman that had accompanied me—this was she! *Hecate.* Her name rose up in my mind.

"I've brought you here to find your secret. Don't fear it child, but yield instead to the truth that can be revealed in the beautiful black."

I got control of my breath, wrapping my arms around myself for support as I beheld her mystical form.

"Tell me, child, what are you most afraid of?"

"I'm afraid that I'm lost!" I cried, but my voice resounded in the vast hollow of the cave and bore down on me like a wave of sound. I gulped at the air, again trying to calm my body, but it was no use. I was shaking.

"*Who* is lost?" her voice was ethereal.

"I am!" I whispered desperately.

"And who are you?"

"Hera, I'm—" but suddenly I wasn't sure what to say.

I felt about myself again, trying to grasp from what direction I had come. I wanted to claim a sense of self by pressing up against another object that was separate from me, but in the darkness, everything merged.

"There are two truths, Hera," Hecate said. "You are your body and all the experiences you have through it. But you are something eternal, as well, which cannot disappear even when your body falls away."

I began to cry softly, overwhelmed by the growing sense of nothingness into which I was merging.

"I'm afraid," I whispered. "I'm so afraid."

"Is that true?" Hecate's voice was warm and full of mirth. "Or is it just your body that is afraid?"

Empty space was all about me, and inside of me, the black absorbed me whole. I was becoming one with it, floating only as awareness, watching the scene unfold.

"You are more than your body, child. Do as I say now, rest in that aspect of you that is so much more! It is time for you to become a woman, a priestess, She who is whole unto herself!"

Quieting my mind as my father had taught me I took control of the terror. Closing my eyes and focusing on my breath I brought my heart and mind together, letting them reach out into the space around me. A sense of peace washed over me. I opened my eyes. The dim image before me smiled, and my body shuddered and relaxed.

"You are immortal, child. You are a body, and you are much more than a body. Awareness is the immortal essence of all things. Everything, good and bad, challenging and joyous is contained within Her womb."

The image of Hecate faded, but her voice continued to fill the space.

"You must live in a world of solid things, but align yourself with your immortal awareness, Hera. Then the answers you seek will be found. You are a fountain of never-ending wisdom. Drink deep child, from your own spring—"

In a moment she was gone, and the dim light she had projected went with her. I sat in the dark and the silence for a long time, but the panic did not return. I stood, slowly, reaching out with my intuition, sensing the right direction to go in. I felt something, like a cool, dim breath on my cheek. A breeze moved over me. I stepped toward it, my face turned into it, skin alert, and hands outstretched groping in the dark. Slowly I moved in the direction of the breeze. My basket and the fine things I'd collected were forgotten behind me. In a few minutes, I stumbled into a trunk and felt its opened lid with my hand. Relief swept over me. I was moving in the right direction. I let my senses continue to pull me, as if by an invisible thread, through the cavern, carefully, step by step.

It seemed like a long time before I felt the cool blast against my face and realized that I'd reached the mouth of the cave. I stumbled outside, righting myself against the enormous boulder that hid the mouth of the cave. I looked up. Stars flickered through the branches above me.

I moved smoothly and quickly about the boulder to the stream and followed its sound through the dark passage of the forest, the brush scratching at my legs and thighs until I came to the little hill and the dim glow of light just beyond. I heard Pegasus's loud whinny, and I stumbled, cutting my knee, but didn't stop, scrambling to the top. When I reached the clearing with the tree, I faltered; Mother stood beside the fire that crackled and leapt before her. She looked up as I broke into the field, her body lurching toward me, her arms outstretched. I ran into them, sobbing. She held me close, rocking gently until I could sit beside her on the mat. She covered me with our blankets and pushed the water bag to my lips, forcing me to drink.

I couldn't take my eyes off the fire, off its beautiful light, and yet inside of it, between the flames, I sensed the immense and unending space and darkness. And I was a part of it. I knew that now. I was not just flesh and bone. Somehow, I was part of *everything*.

Mother pulled a bottle from her bag, from which she poured jasmine oil into her palm and anointed my forehead. Then she pulled me to her again. We sat there together late into the night, the magic all around us, and let the illusions of my substantial reality die away from my eyes forever.

CHAPTER ELEVEN

W<small>E CROSSED THE LAKE</small> to the Emerald Temple in a small boat Mother had found huddled with a flock of others on the shore. The sun was already past its zenith, and the water stretched out before us like a sea. I couldn't see the other side. The center of the lake was shrouded by mist, but as we paddled toward it, Mother chanted, low, under her breath, and bade me shut my eyes. "Imagine a tree, covered with white blossoms, springing up before us," she said.

After a few minutes, her chanting stopped, and I opened my eyes to see that the mist had parted and we moved steadily toward a large isle. Mother guided us to a small, half-mooned bay that was protected from the rest of the island by towering cliff faces and jagged stones strewn across the shore. Far above it, I could make out a tree-lined plateau.

As we neared the shore, two women stood on the beach shading their eyes from the sun. I recognized the younger as Persephone, and she waved to me. The other was older, more of Mother's age, and she stood gracefully on the sand, her hand resting lightly on Persephone's shoulder.

As the craft neared the shore, I leapt out to greet

Persephone and together, we pulled it high up on the beach. The elder woman approached us, a smile on her round face. She reached out her hands to Mother.

"Sophia," she said, her voice filled with the warmth of familiarity.

Mother stepped out of the boat and embraced her.

"Demeter, my friend," Mother replied.

So, this was Persephone's mother. During our travels, I'd heard talk that she was one of the twelve high priestesses that ruled the temple, and served my grandmother, The High Priestess. Demeter was referred to as one of the Twelve Mothers. She wasn't what I'd expected after meeting Athena, whose strong, hard body and manner had been intimidating. Her black robe fell in gentle arcs about her fleshy breasts and wide hips. Her face wrinkled warmly as she smiled. She pressed her hand gently to Mother's cheek then placed her hands together before her breast and bowed slightly. Mother did the same. Then, Demeter turned to me. She reached out her arms and before I could move, pulled me into them. She was shorter than I but soft, and her arms were a comfort.

"Welcome, Hera," she said. "My daughter has told me much about you. We're so happy to have you with us."

"Thank you," I said, "but how did you know we were arriving now, at this place?"

Demeter gave Mother a sideways look, and then the two of them laughed.

"It's an old trick your mother and I used when we were young, slipping from one shore to the other without Rhea catching on. It's an intuitive awareness we learned when we were girls. We'd been so close that we had an uncanny way of hearing the other's intuitive call."

She reached for Mother's hand and squeezed it. They laughed again.

Demeter continued, "Hera, I'm sure you know how to rest in the current you share with all beings. This is the place where your mother and I have always been able to sense one another, especially shore to shore."

I had a thought of Artemis then, a quick flash of the times we'd been afield together, our instincts and timing merging as we moved. This was how she called animals to her, how she joined with some unseen sound, sang to an invisible ear.

Persephone opened a bag beside us and pulled out long white initiates robes. She handed them to us, and I followed Mother's lead by slipping one over my head, letting the hood partially hide my face.

When the robes were on, Persephone approached Mother and bowed before her, kissing the hem of her robe as I'd seen many do to Athena in the days past. While I knew Mother didn't expect it, I could see she was pleased.

"The Lady Athena, is she still on the mainland?" Mother asked.

"Yes, Lady, she waits for you there," Persephone answered. "No one knows you're here, yet."

"Good." Mother looked at Demeter for a long moment then continued, "Take me to the High Priestess."

We left our packs in the little boat, and Demeter led the way toward a sharp, switch-backed staircase that was carved into the side of the rock. She moved easily up the steep incline, her body breathing smoothly, while my own breath became labored. We stopped half way, and I looked down upon the little beach, noticing now that the mist had risen behind us. I could hear the sound of the water lapping gently on the shore, but could no longer see it. We continued in silence.

At the top, I was awed at the vast expanse of the temple grounds. Before us loomed the standing stones, and in the center a small, round building with a high, domed roof that shimmered with copper. Elaborate images were carved into the marble columns that surrounded it. The building glittered in the sunlight.

Mother lifted her hand to her chest as we passed and I saw her bow, slightly, before the solitary tree, filled with white blossoms, which grew before the entryway.

As we followed the path around the stones, we passed a group of women working in a garden. There were others nearby carrying baskets of vegetables on their heads in the direction of a narrow building and courtyard where smoke billowed from a large oven. They hardly seemed to notice us, busy with their work.

"Everyone's preparing for your arrival," Demeter said quietly, leaning toward Mother's ear. "They expect you today, but from the land bridge and with Athena."

"They'll know of our presence soon enough," Mother answered. "I sent our horses on without us. They will reach Athena any time now, and then—" she didn't finish.

The two women smiled. "Athena will not be happy," Demeter said. She put her arm around Mother's shoulder. "It will be alright," she said. "My heart will stand with you, Sophia. You will not be alone."

I had never seen my mother express such natural affection for another woman. I could see how deep her friendship with Demeter must have been by the gentle way caring passed between them.

We moved through a thin grove of trees and entered lush, fragrant grounds that led to a palatial estate set up on a slight rise in the distance. Moving quickly over the cobbled paths, we passed by buildings where women stood high up on ladders thatching roofs, and others laid red tiles. There was a kiln set beside a stone smith's bench, where yet more women fashioned fine bowls and cups from black clay, while others hewed ornate statues from stone. We passed a blacksmith and saw horses running free in the fields beyond. There were fountains with fresh water and large, open buildings where groups of white-robed women sat bent at their looms.

When we came over the ridge, past this busy hub of temple life, I saw the true expanse of the island. A prominent rise was a day's walk directly east, and I could see the width of the valley, lying between two shores. Tall, spindly trees clumped together in the middle, and a thin river ran from the foot of the crest toward them.

We followed closely beside Demeter until we came to the foot of a long, wide limestone stairway that led to the main building's portico. Looking around me, I sensed this was a familiar place and a scene from the waking dream passed before my eyes. I shuddered. Mother reached out and took hold of my arm.

"Are you alright, Hera?"

I nodded, trying to clear my vision.

Demeter stepped ahead of us then, her black robe swirling about her ankles.

"You will follow me now," she said, "a few steps behind. Keep your heads covered and your eyes down. Let them think you're my initiates."

She led us up the stairway in a more relaxed and formal step that we mimicked. There were women with spears stationed at the main entrance, and I recognized the way as we moved carefully up the inner spiral of steps to the landing where the door with the great, carved dragons loomed over me. I shivered when I saw them.

"Calm yourself, Hera," Mother said, but her voice was tense. "You're about to meet your grandmother, Rhea, High Priestess of the Emerald Temple. Stand tall and don't speak unless spoken to."

She gripped my shoulder as she said these last words.

There were more guards at either side of the door, but they nodded in deference as Demeter approached and whispered into the leader's ear. The leader signaled the others, and they stepped away from the doors in unison, pulling upon the large, bronze handles. The doors swung open, and Demeter led us inside.

Everything was as it had been in my dream. Rhea sat in front of the richly decorated altar, her blue eyes piercing and fixed on me. She smiled broadly and leaned toward me as if she would come to me at once, but then she stopped. Her eyes moved quickly to Mother who had stopped several arms lengths from the altar. Demeter and Persephone hung back at the door. Rhea glanced in their direction and waved her hand dismissively.

"Thank you, Demeter," she said, "that will be all."

Mother glanced back at her friend, who looked surprised. But then Demeter smiled warmly at us both as if to say something with her look, bowed slightly, and backed out of the room with Persephone.

The doors closed. We were alone with the High Priestess.

Rhea didn't move or speak, and Mother seemed frozen by my side. I stepped closer to her, slipping my hand into hers. My grandmother's eyes snapped sharply to the movement, resting on our hands' embrace. She looked up at Mother, a strained look on her face.

"So, you lied to me," she said. "You had a girl."

"I had no choice," Mother responded coldly. "You would not have let us go."

Cold anxieties moved over my body as I listened to them speak, and a dreadful knowledge of their painful relationship lit up my nerves. Mother had spoken in a hard, flat tone and though we were shoulder to shoulder, when Rhea stood, her presence seemed to overshadow us both. She moved toward us with strong, regal strides, but her face was soft, her pale skin creased with concern.

"You left me no heir," she said sternly.

"There are others," Mother said, "Persephone has merit."

"But our lineage! The bloodline of the dragon—"

Rhea stopped there, glancing at me. She pursed her lips and shook her head. "Sophia," she began again, more smoothly. "Sophia—" but she didn't finish.

There was a sound at the door and when it was pushed open Persephone stood wringing her hands.

"Forgive me, Reverence," she said, "but word has just come that Athena has found Sophia and Hera's horses. She's sent for reinforcements to begin a search."

Rhea paced back to her chair and sat down with annoyance.

"Send word that my daughter and granddaughter are safe, sequestered here in my house."

"Yes, Reverence," Persephone said, removing herself once again.

Mother remained still beside me. The sounds of a great commotion rose up from the open verandah beside us, and a warm breeze moved through the room. My legs were sore from the long days of travel and riding, and I was exhausted from the journey. I shifted on my feet. Mother squeezed my hand and let it go. She took a step toward Rhea.

"There's not much time now," she said. "I do not intend to be here when Athena arrives."

Rhea slapped her hands down hard on the armrest of the chair, and the serpent heads carved there shaking in her wake.

"I made a mistake, Sophia," she said. "It was a long time ago, and I behaved badly. I was angry and hurt, and I should never have acted from such feelings. Your banishment was a mistake!"

"It was my freedom," Mother said readily, "It was a gift!"

"You were my heir," Rhea said.

"I was in love," Mother responded.

"You disobeyed me!"

"You gave me no choice."

Another long silence and then my grandmother's voice came softly. "Forgive me," she said.

Mother's response was immediate and sharp as a blade. "No."

Rhea nodded and sighed. Her jaw set and her features hardened. Her round, high-set cheekbones and arched brows gave her the look of an owl perched before the midnight hunt. She looked at me.

"The girl looks strong," she said as if I were not there, "and intelligent. She has your lips and your high brow."

"She takes after her father, not me."

Rhea almost sneered at this.

"I will have her initiated immediately, and she can begin her studies—" Rhea began.

"No," Mother cut her off. "I will not let her be initiated before she has a chance to see what her life will be here."

My grandmother was on her feet now and moved toward

Mother fiercely. Mother stepped back instinctively, but did not drop her eyes.

"The Emerald Temple is in danger, Sophia, surely you know that. The politics of the council of Caledocean and the dynasty's priests have shut us out of the expansion efforts. What little voice we have is being lost. Their symbols for the divine are made in male images. They will move into the tribal world with no counterpart, Sophia, just a rich and corrupt priesthood that will offer only one perspective of the divine."

"I will not let her go," Mother said stubbornly.

Rhea looked at me crossly. "Have you nothing to say, girl?" she snapped. "You're old enough to speak for yourself. Do you not wish to know your birthright, to become my heir?"

I hadn't been prepared for this. "I am of age," I stammered, "But I will do what my mother feels is best."

Rhea raised her brow and looked at Mother. "She honors you, Sophia. That is good at least. Guide her wisely in this matter. Give her to the temple and let her take her rightful place."

"In time," Mother said again, "If Hera so chooses."

I was alarmed by the severity of the situation. I hadn't thought that I'd have to pledge to explore my new life. I knew I needed to be here for Mother and Father thought this the only place that could teach me about my unique abilities. Though the fire hadn't risen within me again, and I didn't seem to be able to call it at will, Mother had assured me the ability was true and must be honed, for my safety.

"I must have her pledge, now!" Rhea demanded.

"She's *my* daughter and the temple cannot take her without my permission." Mother declared, stepping forward to face Rhea squarely. "You may have her for three full years, that is all," she said.

I gasped and turned sharply. I looked at her in disbelief but said nothing. Tears rose in my eyes, but I would not let them show.

"Three years!" Rhea cried in outrage as if Mother had slapped her. "While it may not take the girl as long as most, it takes a novice nine years of training, and then nine more in the mystic arts before she's ready for full ordination!"

Mother moved back to my side resting her hand on my shoulder. She spoke calmly now, as much to me as to my grandmother.

"It will not take Hera that long." She paused and looked at me. Her voice softened. "Hera can call forth fire."

Rhea's head snapped to attention at this. Her eyes grew wide, the intense blue fading. She turned and fixed me in her gaze. A warm flush filled my cheeks. When she seemed satisfied, as if she'd read something within me, she looked back to Mother and nodded.

"Fine," she said. "Three years and then Hera will decide for herself."

CHAPTER TWELVE

MOTHER LEFT ME THERE.

She said goodbye on the sequestered beach where we'd arrived, and rowed away from the shore without me. Persephone stood by my side watching as her boat receded into the mist. She put an arm around my shoulders, and I was glad for it. I felt miserably alone.

"You'll have many sisters here, Hera," Persephone said. "You won't be lonely, I promise."

I shrugged and nodded as my mother's thin form disappeared into the mist.

Demeter led us back up the long stairway to the temple grounds. This time, the women noticed us. My pack with my few belongings was slung over one shoulder, and the white robe fit me awkwardly. The hood fell from my face, and my hair spilled unbound from its cords in a thick wave down my back. The strain of the day was upon me; I stumbled at the foot of some small stairs, and Persephone put out her hand to steady me.

"Let me take the pack," she said, but I shook my head.

She looked around at the curious eyes of others staring in our direction and nodded in understanding.

Demeter took me through the busy work area and around the main building that housed my grandmother, the great hall and meeting rooms. From this side, I could see that a large round hall connected the two rectangular wings at the building's center. Below the hill upon which it sat there was a small village, in the distinct shape of a circle. At its center was another round structure, substantial and open aired, and this was filled with girls and women, in short, white robes, chanting.

"That is where we learn to dance, sing and touch the magic of creation," Persephone said pointing to it as we stopped halfway down the hill.

Then she pointed to the big, domed buildings scattered at the perimeter of the village. They were built of stone, with conical, thatched roofs. Some were covered with red, earthen tiles.

"The large halls each have a Mother, a High Priestess in charge of its initiates and their learning," she continued. "Each High Priestess rules over some form of our community life. My mother," she signaled toward Demeter who had stopped a few paces in front of us to let me view the scene, "rules over the house of the earth element. She teaches the use of herbs, and how to use the earth's current in healing with our hands. My mother presides over our fall and spring festivals each year as well." She reached out and squeezed my arm reassuringly. "We live together, you see, as sisters."

Demeter signaled us, and we descended the hill. As we moved through the first row of circular dwellings I was startled to see many young children, boys as well as girls, running about, some playing, while older ones worked at chores. I hadn't realized that the priestesses raised their own children on the island. I knew that they presided over the festivals, as holy women did even in our remote villages, and that they partook in the couplings, but I'd thought that their children must be raised elsewhere. I was annoyed that Mother hadn't shared any of this with me.

Persephone caught me staring. "Women who are pregnant move out of the halls," she explained as we passed, "and into these houses where they raise their children together."

"And the boys?" I asked.

"They stay with their mothers until they are of an age to join their mother's families off the island, and some go to their fathers. It depends on whether the father keeps to the old ways, sharing his mother's house, or has taken up the new form of marriage, and has claimed a house of his own."

Demeter sighed audibly as her daughter spoke this last. "Times are changing," she said.

We moved to the outer circle of buildings and headed toward the one Persephone had pointed out as her mother's. I was relieved to see it, for I thought I would do well under her tutelage, and that the ways of the earth were familiar to me.

My mood sank as we passed her apartments and crossed to the opposite courtyard, which lay on the outermost ring and bordered extensive grasslands. As we neared the hall, I could smell the horses housed within the long, narrow stalls built all about the courtyard. I didn't need either of them to tell me whose house this was. Spears hung over the wooden doors, and the symbol of the double-headed axe was carved into the stone above it, the symbol of the warrior priestess.

"Athena will be your mentor," Demeter said. When she saw my look she reassured me, "It is best this way, Hera, for others may treat you *differently,* knowing who you are in the order of things. Athena will treat you fairly, Hera, and she'll keep you safe. Hers is the house of the warrior, and it's a great honor that she has agreed to take you in."

"Agreed?"

"Each High Priestess accepts only a limited number of initiates into her house. Athena stood up for you before she was sent to find your mother," Demeter replied. "She'll arrive shortly, Hera, and then you'll be asked to pledge your obedience to her for the time you are with us."

I said nothing and dropped my eyes to the ground. The discouragement of my circumstances now rested entirely upon me.

"Come," Persephone said. "You must be hungry and tired."

I said goodbye to Demeter, and Persephone led me into Athena's hall. We passed through the wide, low wooden door and down several steps. Although the walls only appeared to reach to the height of my chin from the outside, the floor was sunk down into the ground so that the internal floor gave the roof an even greater height above me. In the center was a circular ceramic hearth with a thick, bricked column that extended out the center of the roof. An ingenious device, I realized, for keeping the building free from smoke. From the top of the column, plastered beams protruded in all directions forming a circular wheel above us. It was a simple, beautiful sight.

The floor was covered with large, square stones. Sleeping coves were built into the walls all the way around. Tall, wooden trunks were set at the base of these, and Persephone beckoned me to one.

"You'll sleep next to me," she said encouragingly.

My eyes widened. I hadn't thought of her as being in Athena's service. She didn't strike me as the warrior type, and as she wore a black robe, I knew she was already ordained. Persephone was a priestess, not an initiate.

"Why do you serve Athena?" I blurted out, too tired to check my words.

Persephone paused, looking up at me and I was sorry I'd said it.

"I didn't mean to offend you," I began, but she waved her hand and shook her head, a smile still on her face.

"Since my ordination, I've served all the High Priestesses," she said. "It's a good way to be tutored by each of our holy mothers. And it will help me in the future if…" She paused, and for a moment she looked uncertain. She took a breath and continued slowly. "It's always good to know what each house needs and how it can serve the community should one ever take a position of leadership."

I nodded and forced a smile, but I could hear the tension in her voice and resolved not to ask any more questions. She pointed to my pack, and I set it down and pulled out a clean wrap, but Persephone pushed it aside, opening the trunk, and handing me an elegant, white linen tunic with long sleeves and a pair of woolen leggings. She gave me a thick robe into which was intricately woven the design I'd seen on the door outside the hall. The double-headed axe was displayed prominently all along its hem. Persephone moved to the trunk beside mine and pulled a black robe out for herself.

"It gets cold in the evenings," she said.

We took the fresh clothes and moved out the door again, and around the hall to a rectangular building beside it. This was a remarkable pleasure—a bathing house. Inside, the air was hot and moist, and to my surprise, my bare feet were warm on the tiles. I moved toward the sunken tub, which was more like a pool and stripped away my dirty clothes. I stood before the pool and let Persephone pour buckets of warm water over my flesh. She handed me a rough sponge, and I scrubbed away the long, dusty journey. Then I stepped into the pool.

Persephone leaned on a wooden lever periodically and to my amazement and delight hot water gushed in through the hollowed stone duct. It was a new luxury, and I submerged myself in the warm water, letting my muscles relax deeply. Sometime later I reluctantly pulled myself out at her summons, letting her help me dry with a soft, warm piece of cloth. She handed me a vial of rose oil to scent my skin before I dressed. She sat me down on a stone bench and pulled strands of my hair away from my face, wrapping my long tresses about a small, thin stick, tightly knotting it on the back of my head. Afterwards, I stood in the warm beam of sunlight that pierced the open door, and she appraised me and smiled.

"Come along, now," she insisted. "Athena will be here soon, and you need to eat."

She led me outside and farther around the hall to another rectangular building where I smelled hot food and heard the sound of something frying. The kitchen was a big room, and quite grand compared to the small hearths I'd known in my village. The floor was covered with smooth, red tiles, and there was a raised hearth at the far end. Along the walls were big slabs where women stood chopping vegetables and crushing grain. Storage jars as high as my waist lined the wall. Persephone served me a bowl of steaming hot soup and a small mug of wine with water. She handed me a linen napkin, freshly pressed.

I ate heartily of hot bread served to me by a young girl with a slow, sleepy look. The girl watched me as I ate, but said nothing. I shifted uncomfortably on my stool and dipped the last of my bread into the broth. It was delicious, and the spices lingered in my mouth. I drew strength from the meal. When I thought I couldn't eat anymore, the girl handed me a dish with dried dates and cheese, and sweet honey cakes and my appetite was renewed. I looked at Persephone who was laughing at me with her eyes.

"Go ahead," she said, "eat it all. You look as though you need it."

I took a few dates and then pushed the platter away. The girl brought me a bowl of fresh water and indicated that I should rinse my hands. The water was warm, and I wiped my palms on the cloth afterward. From what I could see so far, the work might be hard here, but the way they lived was nurturing and abundant.

There was a loud shout from the courtyard, and the girl went scampering across the kitchen to tend her duties. I heard others gathering outside the window, and Persephone got to her feet. She looked me over approvingly and then led me out into the courtyard where Athena charged in, her women close behind her. She was off her gray before it stopped moving, handing the reins to a young woman without looking at her. She pulled her helmet from her head and tossed it to the girl as well. Then she strode toward me, anger plain on her face.

Persephone knelt on the ground as she approached, and kissed the hem of her robe. I thought it best to do the same, but Athena stopped me.

"No, not you," she said scowling. "They tell me you will not be a full initiate. How can you understand the ritual of obeisance without such a commitment?"

I got to my feet and shook my head.

"I'm only trying to do the right thing," I snapped back. "No one has explained—"

"I will see to that shortly," she said. "Then we'll see what you're capable of."

"I look forward to it," I replied hotly.

Persephone had stepped to the side and shook her head slightly, implying I should be still, but I shrugged her off.

"You know what I expect of you, Hera," Athena went on, "and yet all I've seen is your lack of commitment and loyalty to something bigger than yourself. You seem to care little about the difference such things would make. Sneaking into the temple as you did is just what I'd expect."

"I was following my mother!" I defended but regretted it immediately.

"Oh yes, your mother," she said. "And I hear she has already slunk away."

A large group had gathered around us now, and she punctuated every word.

"Yes, we know what your mother's idea of loyalty is," she finished.

I bit my lip and clenched my fists. She made a small, satisfied sound and then gestured to an older woman who wore a scarlet band about her black tunic, which I guessed noted some form of rank.

"This is Hestia, she tends the hearths and builds the ritual fires. You will assist her."

Then, with a dismissive look, she turned and strode toward the hall of the High Priestess.

The winter and spring of that year moved past me in a blur of activity. I rose early in the morning as I'd always done, but the day began with movement and songs, laughter in the dining hall, and a beautiful camaraderie with the other women and girls. I found myself with a score of sisters, and the old lonely and restless spirit that used to accost me at home was finally banished. I hardly had time to miss my family or the ways of the village life I'd left behind.

After rising and eating we gathered in groups to tend to our ritual prayers and chants. It didn't take me long to learn the ones that they used most frequently, as Mother had already taught me many close forms, and I was well aware of the practice of quieting the mind and turning one's attention to the great indwelling power. I was instructed to go about my day, indeed all of my activities, as the prayer itself, letting the chant vibrate me open to the intimate connection I shared with all beings. Athena instructed me herself. She was more patient then I'd expected, yet very exact. She wanted me aware of this connection in all that I did. In the early months, this was her only lesson.

"Relax your mind and rest in your immortal perception," she instructed. "And one day as you're resting, you will find that your consciousness reaches out and touches the consciousness of another—an animal, a plant, a person—and you will touch the only true power and magic that anyone can possess."

She watched me as I worked. I spent my mornings with the others doing chores, bringing in and storing wood, digging up peat and carrying in buckets of fresh vegetables from the gardens to the various kitchens about the Temple grounds. I often worked in the fields, picking and planting herbs, mixing them as I'd done for Mother, into brews. Once in a while, I would sense Athena, standing on a ridge above me, or hidden in the shadow of a doorframe, watching with her fierce, dark eyes. She didn't interrupt or chastise me as I imagined she would. I assumed, at first, that she was looking for faults in my work. As time went on, however, I became aware that it was not my actions she was studying, but something else, something to do with my instinct and nature.

One night, by the hearth, I moved close to Persephone who sat concentrating on a small piece of embroidery. I asked her what she thought about the way Athena treated me, but she only shook her head.

"The ways of High Priestesses are not always readily understood, Hera. They always have a reason, but you may never know what it is."

I was still uncomfortable. Aphrodite, who had leaned toward the fire with her hands outstretched as if she was warming them, chimed in without an invitation.

"Maybe she doesn't trust you, Hera?" she offered in a tone more pleasant than her words felt.

I'd come to expect such a comment from her by then. Aphrodite was not my friend.

"I've given her no reason not to trust me," I said, "and I work as hard as anyone here."

I heard the defensiveness in my voice and took a deep breath, remembering to rest into the gentle stream of wisdom that was the true nature of my being. I was supposed to speak from this perspective, not my sense of inadequacy. As I tried to relax, Aphrodite shot me a condescending smile.

"Keep practicing, Hera, one day it may come naturally to you—"

Persephone gave her a hard look. Aphrodite shrugged, got up and sauntered across the room. Then Persephone pulled a fresh piece of linen from her bag and handed it to me with a bone needle.

"Put her out of your mind," she said in a hushed tone, "and don't worry about Athena. I think she is not as critical of you as you think. She's been hard on us all."

"But she's always watching me, Persephone, and she pushes me harder than the others. You know it's true!"

She didn't look up from her stitching.

"Everything Athena does is well thought through. If she treats you a certain way, it's for a reason. Athena is wise in her dealings."

"Wise," I mumbled. "That's not the word I'd use to describe her!"

She looked up and sighed as if dealing with an unruly child.

"Hera, Athena is one of the temple's most devoted priestesses. Don't mistake her hardness for uncaring." She handed me a spool of gold thread and squeezed my hand. "She cares much more for you then you think."

I took the linen and thread, smiling at the thought, and to my surprise, I noticed that I hoped it was true. I settled into the quiet rhythm of sewing and let go of the conversation. My mind wandered, as it often did these days, to my tryst with Zeus. He'd been a good lover, and the memory of his magnetic look and the sound of his voice had stayed with me. I wondered if I'd meet him again, but from what I'd gathered of the politics of state his family was not favored by the Emerald Temple. Still, I thought there might be a way to rendezvous off the island at the upcoming solstice ritual in which we'd spend several weeks on the northern shore of the mainland. Though the days would be full of work as we served the people with rituals and healings, the nights would be our own.

Just before the solstice, my grandmother called me to her. Athena escorted me into the High Priestesses' chamber and stood at my side as my mother had once done. The altar burned with solstice candles, and the scent of evergreens filled the room. Rhea looked me up and down. When she seemed satisfied, she moved to her seat and spoke to Athena.

"You say she's coming along well."

Athena's voice showed no enthusiasm. "Well enough, Reverence," she answered.

Rhea nodded as if this was to be expected and then she leaned forward in her chair and said pointedly.

"Hera, you will not be going to the solstice ritual with the others."

My brow rose, and I opened my mouth to speak but caught myself. *Don't react,* I thought. *Take a breath and respond mindfully.*

"Reverence," I began, but Athena cut me off.

"There's plenty for her to do here. She's so far behind the other initiates her age, the time will be well spent."

Rhea nodded and waved her hand as if it was decided.

"But, Reverence," I said, all reserve was forgotten and disappointment evident in my tone.

Athena made a sharp sound and took me firmly by the arm, silencing me. Rhea was shaking her head.

"Forgive my initiate's lack of self-control," Athena said apologetically as she began to step backward toward the door. "As I said, she has much to learn, and the time will not be wasted."

I moved stiffly beside her as she pulled me out of the room. I kept my composure as we walked through the crowded hall and down the stairs but once outside I turned and faced her.

"Lady," I said trying to put a shred of respect into the tone of my voice. "This isn't fair. You're being unreasonable!"

She gave me a hard look but nodded her head.

"Much in life is not fair, Hera. Hard things happen to good people all the time. Good things happen to those who do evil. You can't count on things being fair."

I threw my hands up in the air and turned away, angry.

"It's not right," I said, my voice low. "The solstice is a time of celebration, I've earned that! I've worked hard. I've done everything you've asked of me."

"Not everything," she answered.

"How can you say that?" My voice was low and uneven. "I've left a good life to come here and serve you, but all I feel from you is resentment. Nothing I do is ever good enough for you!"

I turned my back on her, trying to take control of my feelings.

"Hera," Athena responded. She paused, but I didn't answer. I felt her hand on my shoulder, and she stepped in front of me. Grudgingly, I looked up into her eyes. "To all things, there is a season," she said. "The question is not whether you *will* face hardship or adversity. The question is *how* you will face it when it inevitably comes."

She gave me a moment to respond, but I had no words.

"The thing you haven't given is your full commitment," she went on, but her voice was not harsh. "If you step upon a path, give yourself to it. Keep your heart open despite the hardship you will face. An open heart will keep you safe no matter what you face."

Again she waited for me to reply, but I only shook my head and dropped my eyes. I didn't know how to do what she was asking. I felt resentment and a defended heart.

Athena dropped her hand and turned toward the path that led back down to the community.

"Come, Hera," she said finally. "There is much to be done."

After the winter solstice, the weather grew cold, and Olympia's peaks were white capped with snow. We spent more of our time at indoor activities. Many women went to the loom, and some to the potter's wheel, while others tuned to the forges to make tools for tilling, harvesting and building— spades, plowshares and bridles—and weapons for war as well. There was a score of workshops that could supply the community with anything that we needed. Our most precious commodity came from the distillery where we crushed basins of flowers into fine oils for the sacrament of anointing and healing. We traded this for other things, I was told, we might need from the grand houses of Caledocean.

Through this long season, I was sent to serve for short periods at almost all of the workshops, with barely enough time to understand its workings, before moving on to another. In this way, I wasn't given a chance to learn any one skill but took in an overview of how each was connected, and run, and how the goods were used. I became aware that I was being skillfully handled, taught the vast and intricate workings of the community through experience rather than disconnected knowledge. They were grooming me, evidently, to take a place of leadership amongst them. I wasn't sure how I felt about any of this, or if I would ever make the commitment, Athena had spoken of. Since our confrontation before the Solstice, she'd stopped hovering over me. She let others take over my training and given me more freedom within the temple. This meant I was able to spend much more time with the other initiates and priestesses, making friends. By the time spring began I was part of the caring and laughter of a sisterhood. I felt held and valued. I did my best to learn what they taught me, and to be of service to my sisters and the Emerald Temple.

By the end of my first season, I was content enough with my life and training. In the mornings, I assisted Demeter in the house of the healers, anointing the palms of the initiates before they began their work. In the late afternoons, I circled the great halls with Hestia and lit the High Priestess' hearths. It was a simple, time-honored ritual, and I knew that I was privileged to serve Hestia as she was one of the elder priestesses and much respected.

Hestia was very small, her face drawn and thin. She was slightly stooped with age, but she carried herself with dignity, her unbound hair flowing in silver streaks down her back as she walked the outer circle from hall to hall each evening. She was often referred to as 'Mother' although she was not a High Priestess herself. For months, I followed her about, learning the simple calls to the fire element as she lit the hearths with a flint. I found the ritual monotonous, but did not say so, and wondered why a woman from each hall couldn't do the same thing and save us the trouble.

Hestia spoke very little and gave me almost no instruction. The only thing she demanded of me was that I speak the fire prayer, calling forth the fire element before she lit each hearth. I thought little of this, or of my own innate affinity to the fire that I'd shown that day with Artemis and my mother—a day that now seemed a long time ago—for no such spontaneous happenings had occurred since. Instead, I humored old Hestia and smiled mildly at the impotent ritual.

Though I yearned to know much more, I contented myself with the honor of attending her.

Then one evening, after a very long day in the stables with Athena's hard direction and Aphrodite's trite commentary on my performance, or lack thereof, I went wearily to my duty with Hestia. I stood impatiently at her side intoning the fire chant, as we moved from hearth to hearth. When we came to Athena's house, Hestia stopped me abruptly, halfway through.

"No," she said gently, "that is not correct, Hera, begin again."

I took a measured breath. My back hurt from the long day and I wanted to sit down and rest. I repeated the prayer, as women returned from their work, preparing for the evening meal. They moved about us silently and kept their eyes turned away from us in respect. I repeated the chant, and once more, Hestia stopped me. She instructed me to begin anew. My voice had a harsh tone, which I tried to soften, but I recited the words precisely as I'd learned them, sure not to make a mistake so we could get on to the last hearth. Again, Hestia stopped me.

"No, that is not correct, your heart must be one with your words. You must *feel* the prayer, Hera—"

I heard a small laugh at the door. I looked up to see Aphrodite staring at me intently. Her eyes narrowed, and her full lips curled into a smirk. I felt unnerved by her gaze and saw her shake her head when Hestia stopped me once more. I turned to Hestia suddenly exasperated, but she looked up at me evenly and commanded me to do it again. Now, others had stopped what they were doing and watched me as well. Several girls stood by the door, but Aphrodite blocked their way, forcing them to mill about uncomfortably, their eyes wandering in my direction. Exhaustion and spite welled up in me. I felt Aphrodite still gazing at me judgmentally as I persisted in my recital and all the while I thought how I'd like to wipe that look of condescension off her face when there was a sharp sound all about me. A light flickered and then leapt in the hearth, the crackling sound continuing loud in my ears. I felt Hestia step back and heard her call out loudly, but the sound snapped like lightning from my hands, away from the fire and toward the door. I was filled with a sense of power as the heat moved through me, singeing the sleeves of my tunic. The flame leapt in the hearth and then streaked toward Aphrodite who stood stunned at the door. She cried out, throwing up her hands, but it was too late. The fire caught hold of her garment and hair, licking at her face.

Old Hestia was quick to respond. She took my bucket filled with water and doused Aphrodite. A girl beside her took hold of a blanket and batted at the hem of Aphrodite's skirt, which still crackled with orange flame, and another pushed her to the ground, stomping on the hem of her skirt. The other girls ran from the hall, crying out for help.

All the while I stood there and watched, unable to move, horrified, and yet… there was a passionate desire that welled up within me and held me gripped in the heat.

Aphrodite lay on the floor, moaning, as the girls surrounded her.

"My face," she begged, "Not my face!"

I heard Hestia send someone for Athena and Demeter and then she pulled a vial of lavender oil from about her neck and poured the entire thing over Aphrodite's cheek, which I could now see was severely burned, and already ruptured into blisters.

Still, I could not move.

Someone said my name, and there was movement all about me, but no one approached. I stood stiffly, staring as if watching inside a dream. Sweat had broken over my skin, and the heat in my hands was intense.

When Demeter arrived, her eyes grew wide at the scene. She knelt to Aphrodite's side and laid her healing hands upon her forehead, and for a moment, Aphrodite soothed. I could feel the pain receding from her flesh as Demeter touched her. How I didn't know or care. I was aware only that I was somehow linked with Aphrodite, and that the heat that still burned within me wanted very much for the pain to return. The realization frightened me, and yet somehow it was also pleasing.

Aphrodite sat up, pointing her finger at me. "You!" she cried, "You did this to me!"

The women turned then, and all eyes were upon me. I could see by their looks that they were frightened, that what they beheld was not the Hera they'd come to know. The heat stirred again, my body swaying slightly like a flame, and I was dimly aware that I couldn't move away from the hearth. The fire that leapt there seemed to hold me, burning inside me as well.

Athena appeared at the door.

"You're jealous!" Aphrodite spat. "I've seen the way you look at me, the way you envied my relationship with Artemis. You try to steal my beauty—"

"Be still, Aphrodite," Demeter's voice was firm as she motioned for two women to help move Aphrodite to the pillows at the far end of the room.

"Envy!" Aphrodite proclaimed, her face contorting, "You can't stand it that Artemis loves me more!"

I felt my hair move about my face as if a hot wind had brushed it away.

"Aphrodite, be still!"

It was Athena's voice, loud and sharp. Aphrodite stopped, her mouth still open, ready to speak, but then she seemed to see me for the first time, and her voice caught in her throat. She scrambled to her feet with Demeter's aid and moved out the door and into the night. Athena commanded all the girls out behind her. She turned to me then, holding up her hands in a gentling posture. She took a step forward, but stopped abruptly, an uneasy look in her eyes. I felt her reaching out to my mind as she had shown me to do with the horses, but I knew there was no entry. She winced and stepped back, releasing the attempt.

She spoke to me—soft, rhythmic words, kind and friendly, which eased their way into my intellect. Demeter appeared in the doorway again, and then Hestia, and they all spoke in unison, a long, cooling chant, something familiar, something I'd heard before, but couldn't make out through the heat in my head.

Slowly, the warmth diminished within me and their words made sense.

I took a breath and Athena stepped toward me, but the fire crackled as she did. She stopped, waited, then spoke the chant with the others before taking another step. This time, I was able to reach out to her, my eyes burning with hot tears.

Hestia and Demeter moved toward the hearth with pails of water in their hands and doused the fire. As the flame died, so did the power inside of me. My legs trembled, and a wave of nausea moved through me. I swayed uneasily as if I'd faint, but I felt Athena's strong arms about me, easing me gently to the stool, and then all three women laid their hand upon me.

I shut my eyes and wept.

CHAPTER THIRTEEN

THEY TOOK ME TO THE BATHHOUSE and stripped away my clothes, easing my stiff limbs into the tub. Demeter sank into the bath with me, directing me to set my focus on the water and relax my mind. Athena and Hestia left the room. Demeter placed her hand on my forehead, and a cool, sweet sensation swept over my limbs. We sat in silence for some time until I'd collected myself. Then I opened my eyes and inquired about Aphrodite. Demeter's voice was strained.

"I can keep her out of pain until she heals, but—"

Athena opened the door abruptly. She urged us out of the water and handed me a long, white gown and cloak that I obediently put on. She seemed tense, pacing back and forth before the door as I put on my sandals and wrapped my hair high on my head. Short wisps fell about my face, but I had no time to attend them as she beckoned me to follow. I looked from her to Demeter, but both were silent, so I turned and followed Athena out the door.

She took me away from the community, up the long, spiral path to the sanctuary. It was a cold night and the ancient walls of the Emerald Temple—hallowed stones that had been worshipped by generations of priestesses—bore a command-ing and persuasive presence. Athena led me to the small field that stretched out before the temple's entrance, and we paused and kneeled before the sacred tree that grew there. Then she took hold of my arm, guiding me gently, but steadily up the imposing stone stairs, and into our most sacred place.

We passed from one small chamber into another through a door that had been unlocked and opened from the inside. Athena stopped in this room and turned to me.

"These doors only open from the inside," she said in a low tone.

She turned and closed the heavy door behind us and bolted it. The sound echoed through the chamber, and my body shook. Athena reached out a hand to steady me.

"The High Priestess enters through a hidden door with-in the temple itself then unlocks these doors one at a time. There are three chambers, Hera, and we must lock each one behind us as we go, and then signal the High Priestess when we are done. She'll then unlock the one before us, and retreat into the next room. This is how we protect the inner sanctum and what is held within. No one can enter without the High Priestess letting them in."

I tried to calm myself, but I knew I was being exposed to an ancient secret, and I wasn't sure I wanted to know it. I'd never heard of an initiate being taken into the temple before. I had no idea what happened in this place.

When we'd passed through to the last room, Athena moved to the door that led to the final chamber and put her mouth to a hole carved into the wall. She began to chant a short, haunting tune when suddenly I heard the bolt on the other side sliding out of place. Athena stopped singing and pushed the door open signaling me to follow.

The space was just like the one before it. By the half-light of the oil lamps hung from ornate hooks levered into the walls, I saw a female shape waiting for us before the open door at the far end of the room. Firelight danced clearly on the wall of the inner chamber, which was exposed behind her. I felt my body run cold with apprehension. To face my grandmother was an intimidating proposition at any point, let alone on this night, and in this place.

"Reverence," Athena said as we approached.

Rhea nodded and eyed me sharply. Within the shadows of the doorway, her eyes glowed like two full moons as they stared into mine. My body grew tense.

"Aphrodite?" she asked flatly.

Athena shook her head and answered, "She will carry a scar."

Rhea scowled. "I warned you, Athena. I told you to train her mind first!"

Athena's face was grave. "Yes Reverence, but Hestia saw no sign of the ability in the early training, and so I assumed—"

Rhea threw up her hand. "You assumed? And then you took Hestia's word over mine? *Foolish!*"

"Yes, Reverence."

The two women stared at one another. I felt the disappointment move from my grandmother's gaze to Athena. Athena bowed her head.

"As Hera's teacher, you will bear responsibility for her actions."

"Of course, Reverence."

"Tomorrow, before the community you will be judged. That will be all, Athena."

I felt a deep sense of shame. I wanted to speak, but my lips were so dry I had difficulty parting them. Athena knelt and kissed the hem of my grandmother's robe. As she rose, she reached for my arm, but Rhea stopped her.

"Leave Hera with me."

Athena's hand went to my shoulder and tightened there. For a heartbeat, she hesitated. I felt afraid, glancing toward my grandmother's hard, even stare.

"She's not ready," Athena said in a low voice. "I may have misjudged the fire, but I've been watching her closely, and I tell you—"

"She doesn't have to be ready for this," Rhea answered.

Her eyes moved from Athena's to mine and then back again. Dread filled my body.

"Leave my granddaughter with me, Athena. It's the only way to know for sure, and we don't have time to waste. Mt. Olympia *will* erupt, and the flood will come. Truth shall perish if we make a mistake now."

I moved to speak, but Rhea caught my eye with a stern look. I closed my mouth and lowered my eyes instinctively. Athena straightened, dropping her hand from my shoulder. She turned back the way we'd come, but before she stepped forward, she reached out and touched my chin gently, tilting my head back up to look at her.

"My heart shall stand with you," she said softly. "You will not be alone."

I remembered Demeter speaking these words to my mother the day we arrived, and I felt the strong sense of protection from Athena as she spoke them now. I nodded and tried to smile. Then she moved away from me. She passed back through the door, and my grandmother bolted it behind her.

I was left alone in the presence of the High Priestess of the Emerald Temple. The fact that she was my grandmother did not make me feel any safer. In the many months, I'd been on the isle, I'd only met with her on a few occasions, and those had been awkward at best. Now, I felt utterly stricken in her company.

She took an unlit torch from the wall and stepped into the inner sanctum. I turned and followed, haltingly.

The room was much larger than it appeared from the outside. A fire blazed in the large, open hearth. I stopped short when I saw it, but my grandmother took hold of my elbow, firmly pulling me forward.

"It's alright, Hera," she soothed. "You will not call up the fire in this place."

There was a strange, uneven hue to the things around this room and I sensed my grandmother's strong magic. For a moment I thought I should stop, deny her instruction, and run from the temple, but where would I go and to whom? I had to learn how to control the fire before I hurt someone else.

I shook off the thought of fleeing and followed her lead. She lit the torch in the flames and lifted it in the air. I watched the smoke rise up into the domed ceiling and out a hole in the center through which I could see the silver crescent of the moon. We moved toward one of the walls and she shined the light upon it. A mural was painted there, with mosaic tiles set about it making pictures that told the story of the island of Lemuria, the homeland of most Atlanteans. It was an elaborate portrayal of the priests and priestesses fleeing the flood of their island home and their arrival on the shores of Atlantis.

"Many things have changed since then," she said. "There was a time when we honored the invisible life force without giving it a form. But that time has come and gone." I heard resentment in her voice. "Now the priests have given a face to that which is faceless! A *male* face, Hera, with male attributes. They are re-imagining the divine in their own image."

"But why?" I asked.

"For power and control," she answered. "Priests control the kings, and the kings control the armies and armies, well—" she paused and looked again at the image on the wall.

As she walked the circular room the flame revealed the images of centuries past. These were scenes of the Great War, when the priests united the clans and anointed kings who in turn built for them the commanding temples of the central city, Caledocean. Cut deep into the rock and painted with ochre and crimson were icons of people moving from their tribal communities, into the city, and building large ships that sailed forth into the unknown waters of the world.

As we moved about the room, I noticed deep holes receding into the crevices of the black stone. The holes were scattered with no apparent aim, some wide mouthed and others narrow. I could feel my grandmother watching me as I sought the purpose of these gaps. She slowed before an image of a great serpent. Wings lined with gold branched out from its back and rubies were set in place for its eyes. Its mouth was a large, open cavity lined with crystals that glistened red in the reflection of the flame.

"Draconis," my grandmother said, her voice taking on a low and spellbinding note. I'd heard that tone used before when Artemis had called the boar, and a chill ran over my skin. I found myself staring at the open mouth in the wall against my will.

A memory came to me then, sharp and clear, of Mother holding me as a child, while a thin, brown snake slithered across our path. She had leaned down and, to my delight, the snake had moved toward her, a long line of grace, and wrapped itself about Mother's arm and rested there as we continued on our way. She'd taught me one of my favorite hymns that day, of the snake priestesses of Lemuria, who had escaped the flood and founded the first Emerald Temple here on Atlantis. They kept to the old ways of the Mother communities while the priests created a new archetype of power.

I heard a passage from the song ring out through the hallowed room before I realized it was my own voice singing it:

Thirteen priestesses crossed the sea
To hold peace in the face of priestly strife
They built their temple of emerald and gold
To house the serpent-oil of immortal life

I blinked hard and my eyes watered. Rhea was staring at me with a satisfied look on her face.

"Your mother taught you the legend," she said warmly.

She turned back to the wall and pointed at the gold, engraved vial that rested in the serpent's coils.

"Each of the thirteen priestesses founded a house of learning and took control of a holy oil that opened the senses of the body to receive medicinal properties and intuitive strength. The thirteenth priestess, a woman of our lineage, went beyond the distilling of medicine and brewed an oil of the dragon blood plant and the serpent's venom and things unseen."

She stopped there and pointed to the picture on the wall of a woman, her body transfigured, surrounded by light. I thought of the last verse of the song and spoke it.

The oil released upon her head
The light, the light she became
Trapped in a physical cage
Of her body, she will always remain

Rhea nodded. "The thirteenth priestess anointed herself and transformed her body into an immortal form, a perpetual prison of her vast consciousness. While she had mastery over the seen world, she couldn't release herself from it. When the priests discovered her perpetual life, they coveted the oil. They rose up against the Emerald Temple to seize control of it, but the thirteenth priestess reached out to the mist, found its language and wrapped us all in its walls of protection."

I turned to her, gripped by the story.

"And the oil?" I asked. "Does it really exist? Is it here?"

My grandmother nodded.

"Yes, child, the oil is real, and it cannot be destroyed. The immortal priestess tried to give it to the earth, burying it beneath the tree you see outside this temple, but the tree flowered within days of the oil's placement and it has never ceased since. Through all the seasons, Hera, the white blossoms remind us of the power we are responsible for. When the priestess tried to destroy the alabaster jar that held the oil, she found it would not break, and when the oil was poured into another container, the alabaster jar replenished itself."

I looked back to the wall and the images engraved there. I caught the faint movement of a figure on my left side. I snapped my head around, but when I looked it was gone. In another moment I saw it again, now on the right of me, flat and shiny against the wall, but again, it disappeared. My grandmother moved very close to me, her hand resting gently on my shoulder.

"A time will come, Hera, when Atlantis, too, will fall in a quake and a flood, and it is said that we will know that time is near, by a sign. A woman of flame and the holy blood shall rise from the common folk, and she will come to carry the dragon's blood into the world in safety. She will become the living temple, and upon her neck it will rest, protected from the greedy, ignorant hands of those that would use it for power."

I felt my hand rise from my side, watched it move forward toward the carved serpent's mouth. I had a distinct sense that something lived inside this wall—something long and old that slithered down throats of stone. As I stepped forward and reached for the crystal flames, the illusion of warmth and life, a dim thought crossed my mind that I should not do this; I should turn and run. Instead, I moved forward a step and placed my hand inside the hole.

My grandmother now seemed far away, a muted drone sliding into the hollow of my mind.

"Before the thirteenth priestess left us, she anointed an asp and set it here in these stones to protect the oil and our history. When the woman of the prophecy comes, the asp will acknowledge her, and she will become the Draconigena, the Dragoness of Atlantis. She will keep the oil of immortality safe, and through her, the wisdom of the Emerald Temple shall live on."

My hand shook. All reason had abandoned my body as I thought to step away, but my legs would not move. I watched, as the serpent appeared before me, its mouth open, and fangs exposed. Its eyes seemed to be two beads of obsidian black reflecting my own. I was transfixed as the snake's body slid out of the carved serpent's mouth and bound itself to my arm. My heart recoiled, but my arm remained outstretched. In one rapid movement, the asp coiled up my arm and wrapped itself neatly about my neck, its soft, forked tongue hissing in my ear.

"I am Medusa—" I heard the name rise within me and felt the succulent body tighten so that the veins in my neck pulsed hard against my skin. "And you are the Draconigena—"

A vision rose before me, and I swayed. It was a woman with inked skin and dark hair that was long and unbound, her eyes brightened, like a creature of the night. She pressed her mouth to a hole in the stone wall toning a deep and ancient sound that filled the space. Movement flashed from every opening, a sleek and sensuous undulation, like the creature that held me in its grasp. The woman's sound had called the serpents to her. She laughed, as I perceived this. Placing her hands on the stone walls, iridescent snakes coiled up her forearms, draping themselves over her shoulders. As she turned to me, I shuddered.

"I can't be the Draconigena," I said. "I don't have the strength. I'm still so afraid," I spoke into the vision, and the woman softened and answered.

"Of course you are, dearest, you're still so young."

"I want to be ordinary," I said, "I want to live an ordinary life!"

"You will never live an ordinary life, Hera, no priestess ever really does."

The snakes lifted their heads and hissed, the sound echoing around me.

"I can't be the Draconigena," I said. "I don't know how."

"You *will* do this," she said. "But, there will be more to your life as well. There will be love and children too. You will always feel your purpose like a river inside of you, and the current will pull at you until you give yourself to it."

She reached out her hand and opened her palm. There lay the alabaster jar holding the oil of immortality. I could feel it pulsating, throbbing, beckoning me to reach out and take it!

"Hera, every being is living two stories. One is the story of their lifetime, the story of their flesh and bone. The other is their sacred story, the story of their eternal self, She who will never die. For you, dearest, it is the sacred story that shall always come first. That is your calling, Draconigena!"

As I watched the scene, the serene and delighted look on the woman's face drew me in, closer and closer. As she swayed, I swayed, and all my fear left me.

"Draconigena," the woman whispered. "My heart stands with you."

The vision faded and the pressure around my neck relaxed. The asp slid gently to my wrist, wrapping itself about me in a slow, contented fashion. I could feel her quiet strength against my skin, and somehow I knew that she was mine. My head swooned. I knew I would fall, but before I did, I heard a voice again—my own. "I am the Draconigena," I said.

I awoke the next day in my grandmother's chambers. Athena sat beside my bed, a black streak of clay across her forehead. I winced when I saw it, knowing it was the mark of her shame and that she would wear until the next full moon. She sat quietly beside me and reached out a kind hand when I turned toward her, but something moved against my arm, and the asp rose up to face her. I didn't react, but Athena pulled back her hand quickly and stiffened. A strong sense of peace moved toward me from the creature as it wavered in the air and then sank back down and resumed a comfortable place about my wrist.

I reached out and ran the fingers of my other hand over the snake's skin, and an incredible warmth moved through me.

"Medusa," I said her name quietly as I lifted my arm.

She moved smoothly back up my forearm and beneath my gown laying herself lazily about my neck. I laughed, delighted by the sensations of her movement against my skin, all apprehension replaced by wonder.

"You will get to know each other well, Draconigena, and she will never harm you," Athena said, reaching out to take my hand again. "She will keep you safe, and you'll learn to communicate with her as you do with the horses."

I was startled by her soft tone and surprised at the relief I felt in seeing her. I began to tell her what happened in the temple, but she held up her hand.

"There will be plenty of time for us to talk, Hera, but now, we must go." She handed me a plain, linen tunic and a hooded cloak. "Put these on."

I slid out of bed and changed. Medusa coiled herself warm about my waist, hidden from sight and I thrilled at the sensation and closeness.

Athena pointed to a plate of honey cakes, and a cup of warm milk set out on the little table by the window. I took a seat and began to eat heartily.

"Good," she said, taking the seat next to me. "You need to regain your strength."

I nodded pushing another piece into my mouth then drinking down the mug of warm milk beside it.

"Where are we going?" I asked as I took the last piece of bread.

She took a long, slow breath, her shoulders sagging.

"We have to leave, Hera," she said slowly.

I put down the bread, nodding my head. I stared down at the table.

"Of course," I said. "She's sending me away."

She reached out her hand. "Not to punish you, Hera, but to keep you safe."

I nodded again, but I could not meet her gaze.

"I'm going to take you somewhere safe, to a teacher who knows more than any of us here. She will train you in the mystic arts. She will give you the skills to control your... *gift.*"

"My gift," I repeated. "That's all my grandmother wants from me, isn't it? That's the only part she loves."

"Oh, Hera," Athena said leaning in close, shaking her head. "Your grandmother is the High Priestess, and she must do her duty before all else. That's something you're going to have to learn before you become..."

I looked up into her eyes, but she didn't finish.

"Come, it's getting late, we must go," she said, rising from the chair.

I followed Athena out of the chamber and down the stairs. There were no guards and no women anywhere. We moved down the corridor and out into the courtyard unseen.

My horse Pegasus and Athena's gray stallion were tethered by the gate, which opened to the long, narrow land bridge that would take us across the lake. The saddlebags on Pegasus were full. I looked at Athena in dismay.

"You've already packed my things? You're making me leave without saying goodbye!"

"No, it is only that we must leave unseen for your protection. No one must know when, or where we are going. There are forces at work that would not want to see you hone your intuitive gifts, Hera. Surely you understand that."

"I understand."

She pulled up the hood of her cloak and bid me do the same. My body stiffened with resentment, but I did as she instructed.

She mounted the gray stallion and headed toward the land bridge. I followed on Pegasus close behind her, glancing over my shoulder at the great hall on the hill. I could hear the sounds of the community on the other side, the vibrant bustle of life, the voices of my sisters carrying in the wind and I longed to be with them.

Then, something else caught my eye. On the hill above us stood the lone figure of my grandmother. She raised her hand above her head. Then we disappeared into the mist.

We traveled undercover, and by night when the moon would lend us her light. When we reached the Western shore, we skirted the remote villages, until we came upon an ancient grove that grew just beside the sea. I felt the power of the place long before we reached it. Thick Banyan trees spread out their ancient limbs, entwining with one another like old lovers. A thin trail, overgrown with shrubs and blackberry vines, wound its way up the hill behind the grove. Spring flowers grew in rich patches of blossom all along the incline that led to the cave of Hecate, priestess of the cycles of life and death—my Teacher.

The Story Continues in
HIGH PRIESTESS OF ATLANTIS
Book Two of The Priestess Chronicles
Available Now At:
www.JulienDuBrow.com

For more information about the author and Sacred Healing
or to receive updates on Julien's new books and offerings sign
up for her newsletter at: www.JulienDuBrow.com

AUTHOR'S NOTES

In writing this book, I have explored a myth-making process in which I imagined a time before the concept of God existed. I've always wondered what compelled our species to create the concept of an all-powerful being or beings, and I've often pondered how this being became gendered. As a scholar of mythology and mysticism, I've found that the oldest texts, songs, hymns and sacred poetry from around the world refer to an experience of unity as the primary and enduring reality. Even the mystics symbolize their experiences through gender and analogy. Thus, in writing my own myth, I've presented the central divine experience as unity and used the Minoan and Mycenaean cultures that lived 2600-1100 B.C. to create an entirely fictional time-period, in a setting that lives somewhere between myth and reality.

While it is a work of fantasy I've used the storylines of western culture's Greek Pantheon to craft this tale and in so doing, I feel it is important to share a brief description of their creation story and the true origins of their Goddess, Hera. The primary sources of the information below are Edith Hamilton's book, *Mythology*, and Vicki Noble's groundbreaking book, *The Double Goddess*.

Greek Mythology:

Ancient Greek civilization is generally acknowledged as the foundation of western culture. The Greeks reached a high level of sophistication in their philosophy, art, science and political life. The aspect of their civilization that intrigues me the most is their mythology, which pervaded their daily lives. Many of their myths date back to the pre-Greek cultures. These people lived in a matriarchal society and worshiped the Great Goddess, or Earth Mother, who represented fertility and the cycle of the seasons and the wondrous mysteries of life and death. This goddess had a consort who was linked with the starry heavens and who became the Sky God, Zeus. The Great Goddess was then Hellenized by the Greeks into the goddess Gaia, and her daughter Rhea.

The Greek Creation Myth:

In early Greece, the mythology was handed down by a strong oral tradition, until the time of Hesiod's *Theogony* in the eighth century BCE. Hesiod's telling of the Greek creation myth begins with Gaia, the Great Goddess of the earth emanating from Chaos, and thus the world begins. Chaos also births Uranus, the embodiment of the sky. Gaia and Uranus then mate. They have many offspring, two of which are Rhea and Kronos. Uranus devours his offspring until his son, Kronos, outwits him. Kronos mates with Rhea, and also devours his offspring until his son, Zeus, outwits him. Zeus then marries his sister, Hera, and divides the universe into three parts, giving his elder brother, Poseidon the sea, his brother Hades the underworld while he becomes the ruler of heaven and earth.

Hera:

Hera has been portrayed in western culture as Zeus's wife and sister. She was raised by the Titans Oceanus and Tethys, and Ilithyia (or Eileithyia) was her daughter. In Greek mythology, she is presented as the protector of marriage and married women, and most accounts describe her as a jealous wife with a wicked temper and very little compassion.

This is the image that the western world has perpetuated of the queen of the gods, and yet, in my research, I've found that this couldn't be further from the truth. Recent archeological finds now make it clear that Hera *predates* Zeus. She was venerated long before the sky god appeared. It is now thought that the worshipers of Zeus conquered the early Greek tribes that worshiped the goddess, and had their sky god (Zeus) marry the mother goddess (Hera) in order to bring him into the people's new worship. Over time, Greek authors change Hera's role of beloved mother protector to that of a jealous wife.

Before Zeus, Hera was known as the double goddess, the mother, nurturer, and wisdom keeper. Somos was the Greek isle dedicated to her teachings, and her temple still stands there today.

Although the Greeks consistently tell stories of Hera's angry nature, they couldn't hide how deeply venerated she was. We see this primarily in the fact that there are more temples built in her honor throughout Greece than any other god or goddess.

When reading the mythological tales of Hera, and comparing them with the evidence of her superior worship and ancient status, I couldn't help but notice that the Greek men writing their culture's histories had changed and maligned the character and stature of this mother goddess. This led me, and my storyline, to the usurper god, Zeus, and his motives for changing Hera's true story. Their relationship mirrors the fall of matriarchic living and the rise of patriarchy in the western world. Also, it gave me a backdrop to explore the remarkable invention of the God and the Goddess.

ACKNOWLEDGMENTS

I give thanks to my remarkable family and friends. You have held me through my own journey of healing and awakening. You have been a light in my life, and I am deeply grateful.

To Martin, who has stood by side in the light and dark moments of my life, holding up the torch of love that has so often been my guide… thank you, dearest. With all my heart, thank you.

To my teachers, I bow in gratitude for the gifts you have so generously given. I carry your teachings, your strength, and compassion within me, forever. Thank you.

And to all who will read these chronicles—I thank you for your support and wish you love and kinship on your journey.

My heart is with you.

Julien